Christopher Tull was born in 1936, the son of a country rector. Ordained in 1962, he spent all his ministry in parishes between Tiverton and South Molton in rural Devon. Now retired, he still lives in the West Country and remains active in church life.

His previous publication, *Challacombe The Story of an Exmoor Village*, has been highly praised. It is available through bookshops and Broad Street Publishing.

Also by Christopher Tull

Challacombe The Story of an Exmoor Village

Forthcoming Titles

Greener Grows the Grass?
The Green Grass of Summer

IN PASTURES GREEN?

Christopher Tull

BROAD STREET PUBLISHING

Printed and bound in Great Britain by
Short Run Press Limited, Exeter

BROAD STREET PUBLISHING
Arden Cottage, Coombeshead Road, Highweek,
Newton Abbot TQ12 1PZ
Tel +44 (0)1626 365478
Fax: +44 (0)1769 573350

For
Leslie and Evelyn Tull
and
Ronald and Grace Herniman
whose teaching and example have meant so much
to me in my ministry

*   *   *

I would also like to express deep appreciation

To my daughter, Elizabeth, who typed many of the chapters and
started me on a word processor

To Norman Dallyn, who also helped me with my word processing

To Chrissie and Mark Young of Broad Street Publishing
for their dedication to publishing my book

To Jiff Booth for kindly allowing me to use her original
watercolours for the cover illustration

And last, but not least, to my wife, Rosemary, for painstakingly checking
all my work and for coming up with good ideas when I got stuck

Chapter 1

Uncle Tiddly

"It can't be, no, it can't be!" cried our children together. "It is. It really is, it's Uncle Tiddly!" I was answering the phone in the kitchen at lunch time. The Longfield family was half way through steak and kidney pie, served up with the first potatoes harvested from our rectory garden.

Mary, my wife, was looking horrified. Her brown eyes glared at me from under her dark curly hair. It was her cousin, Will's, booming voice, on the other end of the line. Already I could smell his beery breath and the stink of stale tobacco which always seemed to emanate from his clothes. Eight-year-old Paul was thoroughly enjoying the phone call. His round face lit up as he began to pull faces in imitation of 'Uncle Tiddly', the nickname he'd given Will.

Ann, Paul's sister, was a year younger. She hesitated, unsure at first how she should react. Then she joined in the fun, her ponytail bobbing up and down with delight.

Will continued on the telephone. "I've got something important to ask you. Could arrive at Leighford Station at 4.15pm tomorrow afternoon if that's OK?"

"No!" cried Mary overhearing this.

"Promise you I'm a reformed man. Won't touch a drop of drink the whole time I'm with you. So sorry about what happened last time."

With all the noise going on behind me, it was hard to make the whole thing out. Did I detect slurred speech? Even if I did, it was such a cry from the heart. Evidently this time he really had an important

1

reason to see me. I hoped in some way I could help him. As a medical orderly during the war I'd helped a good many servicemen with drink problems.

"All right, I'll meet you." I put the telephone down and prepared to face the wrath of my wife as once the early Christians faced the lions.

"After what he did only six months ago," cried an anguished Mary. "When the bishop instituted you here! How can you invite him back, even if he is my cousin? You're too soft hearted, Jack! It's bound to end in disaster. Visits from Will always do."

Mary was normally such a calm, collected person. Born thirty-five years ago, she was brought up in the rectory of the small Wiltshire town of Towchester, and seemed to sail through the troubled waters of parish life. I was still new to many of the traumas facing clergy. Normally I found Mary's manner very reassuring, but there was another side to her and at the prospect of Will's visit her face hardened and there was war in her eyes.

"But we like Uncle Tiddly," Paul and Ann chorused, beaming all over their faces. Their enthusiasm did not altogether help my situation.

"He's full of fun and jokes." Paul persisted, laughing away. "You should have seen the bishop's face when Uncle Tiddly told him you were worth a dozen of them!"

"If he'd left it there it might not have been so bad. But when he went on about the bishop and the barmaid!" Mary threw her hands up in despair.

Fortunately the bishop had assumed Will was some fan from my old parish. A coach load of them had come over to join the crowd at the Institution Service which marked the beginning of my ministry at Ashenridge. The party included my old vicar, Algernon Wright, who had never forgiven me for abandoning the real work of the church which he considered lay in the towns, not the comfortable green pastures of old England.

"Anyway that does it. I'm off to London to stay with my sister. I've been promising to visit her for months."

"Fine," I replied, rising to the occasion. "And I'll get the booze in and we'll have a party!"

Over the cooler atmosphere of tea I explained that Will really did sound as though he had a good reason to see me, and seemed genuinely sorry about his last visit. Mary was none too convinced about this. However, after she'd calmed down a bit she decided it was not essential to go to London. For their part, the children looked very disappointed about Uncle Tiddly's reformation. They did not want to picture him as a lost sheep returning to the fold.

*   *   *

Next morning I awoke to a breathtaking scene. Below us the Badger Valley was shrouded in mist, while our village was bathing in the early morning sunshine. As I gazed over to the hills opposite, it looked as if we were floating on a sea of milk. I sensed a hint of autumn in the cool air as I went outside to admire the garden into which we'd put so much time during the summer.

Unfortunately, the finest display of flowers had nothing to do with us. It was the work of Reg Pert. In the days of my elderly predecessor, Reg enjoyed the run of the entire grounds in exchange for supposedly keeping it in order. After we moved in, he'd reluctantly agreed that a two-acre, overgrown garden was large enough for both of us to share. We thought he'd be pleased to see the old garden come back to life as he watched Mary and me slowly clearing away all the brambles. Instead he looked on in dismay. Then we discovered why. He had deliberately left most of the rectory garden wild to conceal his bed of prize dahlias from prying eyes. He timed his growing so that they were at their peak for the village flower show held at the end of August. His beautiful yellow flowers looked worthy of Kew Gardens.

For all Reg's efforts, the champion dahlia grower in the village was actually Ned Hooper. Ned had none of Reg's inhibitions about displaying his prize blooms. They flourished in his front garden for all to see. Directly behind them, sitting on the windowsill, sat the cup he had won for the last four years. Ned was not known for being brief over what he had to say, and people were getting tired of being way-laid as they passed his gate. They would be held captive for ages as he boasted about his dahlias. He assured everyone that he would win the cup again this year.

"Mind you shut the gate," he would say to visitors as they eventually escaped. "Just make sure 'tis really shut."

The result of all this was that most people wanted Reg to win this year. It was not simply that people were weary of Ned's bragging. If he won the cup for a fifth time he would be entitled to keep it, and the Flower Show Committee would have to buy another one which it could ill afford.

As the day of the flower show approached his excitement was reaching fever pitch. Now he knew where Reg grew his flowers, he kept sending his scouts round to see them. More and more of his pals were finding excuses to come into our garden.

The only other serious competitor was my churchwarden, Colonel Waters, but a misunderstanding about who was to water his dahlias while he was away on holiday effectively ruined his crop. The poor things had simply curled up and died.

"Just as well," Reg commented to us. "What with they fancy tubers 'e buys up country."

This year Mary decided to enter the competition. She was trying her hardest in her newly restored flower bed. Reg would inspect her humble efforts with a look of contempt. It was bad enough this wretched rectory family wanting its garden back, but now that woman had the cheek to grow dahlias for the show. Yes, a woman, too! This really was adding insult to injury. Still, she had no chance of winning.

Our family was not to be put off by the likes of Reg Pert. Country people place a lot on their clergyman caring for his garden and grow-ing things well. That was why we were doing it, not for the prizes. The more he carried on, the more determined Mary became. Reg muttered about petals being uneven, or Mary's timing being all wrong for the show. Then one day he was delighted to spot earwigs, which he pointed out were spoiling the flower heads. She'd got so irritated

I suspected her real reason for not going to London was because she didn't want to miss the flower show.

*   *   *

The atmosphere at lunch the next day grew thicker and thicker. I remained quiet but apprehensive. Was I being a fool? An easy touch for a penniless Will? Mary tried not to notice the excited state of the children as they waited for the storm to break.

"Will he be wearing his yellow suit with soup stains down the front?" asked Paul.

"And what about those naughty joke books?" added Ann. "Do you think he'll let me see them this time? Anyway, what does he do for a job? I think he's a secret agent."

"Nonsense," said Paul. "He sells naughty books at markets. Dad, is he going to bring his housekeeper? He says she's a smasher."

"No, that wasn't his housekeeper, that was his wife. Anyway, what's the difference between a housekeeper and a wife?" asked Ann.

I was not going to get entangled in that one, so I passed it off with a laugh. When Paul started telling me about a tie displaying a naked lady which fell out of Will's suitcase I felt it was time to change the subject, and thankfully it was time for me to drive to the station.

*   *   *

Out of the pull-and-push steam train that terminated at Leighford stepped a truly impressive Uncle Tiddly. He was a fine-looking man, substantially built, with greying hair and a curled moustache. He looked really dashing in his white flannels and striped blazer. He wore a white shirt and red bow tie, and his head was graced with a large Panama hat. His fingers were stained with nicotine, but there wasn't a whiff of alcohol about him.

"Here I am!" he announced. Then as I took his suitcase from him, he stretched out his arms in a grand theatrical pose and addressed as many people as happened to be within earshot. "William the Terrible," he declared. "Returning to the fold like the Prodigal Son." Each word, each syllable was clearly and carefully enunciated in a huge resonant voice. "How good, how wonderful to see you all again."

As we drove off he regaled me with stories about all the latest plays in London, which bore a striking resemblance to the reviews printed in the papers. Then he told me about a wonderful hair conditioner. *The cure for baldness and all scalp troubles.* So that was what he was up to. Trading in quack medicines. He carried on about cures for warts, backache, lumbago and headaches, almost as if he was standing in the market place rather than sitting in the family car.

As the journey continued I detected a strange odour. At first I couldn't think what it was, then I recognised it as the familiar musty smell of jumble sales. Was that where he bought his clothes?

* * *

Posters and flags at the entrance to the village reminded us of the flower show on Saturday. Entering the drive I passed Annie Cook, who apparently found it necessary to go all the way round our garden to deliver a note. Annie never missed a thing. She was blessed with a sharp chin and had a habit of pointing with her slightly crooked finger. In the summer months she wore an old print dress for gardening, short boots and a battered sun hat. When I first met her I thought that black clothes and a pointed hat would have suited her better. As I got to know her I realised I was quite wrong. Her curiosity could be a bit annoying, but she meant well, and over the years she proved to be a great help to me.

Annie was one of a succession of keen gardeners who, on one pretext or another, just happened to go past Reg Pert's now exposed dahlia bed. Things were hotting up for Saturday.

* * *

I was soon made to look a fool. The only reason for Will's visit was simply to ask me to sign his passport form. I tried to find out exactly where he was going. I asked him . . . I teased him. All I got was 'A rolling stone gathers no moss'. Then suddenly he amazed the whole family by announcing that after his continental tour he would be exploring new avenues of commerce in this part of the world. To my horror I pictured him setting up in Leighford Market on a Wednesday morning selling medical cures of dubious worth to our local farmers.

Apart from this news, and a house filled with tobacco smoke, Will's first evening with us was a great success. Once the children got over the disappointment of his not being the worse for wear, they realised he was even more fun with his stories and card tricks. Even Mary relented. He ate magnificently and gave her high praise for her cooking. As for drink, there was not a suggestion of it. He seemed quite happy with coffee and biscuits.

Had we misjudged him? Could he keep it up? Or did he have a bottle of something in his bedroom?

Chapter 2

The 'Haccident

Whatever Will may or may not have drunk the night before, he slept like a log. Loud snores could be heard at nine o'clock, heavy breathing at ten, and it was only when the children accidentally banged against his door during a friendly scrap that he woke. Hearing the noise I rushed upstairs. At that moment Will burst out of his bedroom and before I could say a word he was in the bathroom. The children were quite taken aback to see Will without his genial facade, and it required no words of rebuke from me to send them scurrying into a far corner of the garden.

The sun came out and so had Will's smile by the time he appeared downstairs. Before long, Paul and Ann learnt to do several conjuring tricks, heard a hilarious story about hunting in the jungle, and were now studying the ancient art of playing chess.

This same sun also encouraged a group of hungry sheep to break out of a field and wander through the village until they found an open gate. There were rich pickings from the garden inside. Unfortunately, despite all his warnings to others, Ned himself must have left his gate ajar when he went out that morning. Perhaps he'd been trying to find out the latest news about Reg's flowers. The first thing we knew about it was when Reg appeared with a look of triumph all over his face. He could hardly wait to tell us about Ned's trampled dahlias. Now he was bound to win the cup.

That afternoon I managed to adjust the times of a couple of meetings so that I could take Will for a drive over the moor. Mary deliberately kept the others near the car picking whortleberries while Will and I went for a stroll. A world of purple heather lay at our feet. Above us a lark sang, and on the horizon buzzards glided in the warm air.

"The trouble with you padres is that your life is too easy," he said, supposing I had nothing better to do that afternoon than go for a walk. "Just look at all you've got. A nice home, family, friends, never a day's care. If my marriage had been like yours . . ."

Then his voice suddenly changed. "But come on, wicked William, it's no good talking like that. No good feeling sorry for yourself."

And he didn't. Instead he gazed all round him and began conjuring up fantastic ways of converting this wild moor into what he called 'a proper commercial enterprise'. Oh yes, he could see his way to making a fortune here.

This was part of Will's problem. He lived in a make-believe world where he was always the hero. In real life he'd allowed himself to become a rather pathetic character. He'd arrived at my house with almost no money, jobless, and leading a seemingly purposeless life. What sort of existence was that for a man in his fifties? In his youth he'd been expelled from a minor public school. He later showed some talent as an actor, but after various unsatisfactory jobs in the world of entertainment he fell for a 'hostess' at a notorious London nightclub. His father refused to have anything to do with the marriage and his family more or less disowned him.

After relieving him of such money as he possessed, his wife abandoned him for someone else. At the beginning of the Second World War he joined up, but not a word was heard from him until well after the war had ended.

As we strolled along we talked a little about the war years. "Those were my finest days. I volunteered for dangerous work, and by Jove I got it. I was parachuted behind enemy lines and worked with the resistance." Will's voice became choked with emotion.

Moved by what he was saying, I encouraged him to go on. I told him he was no fool. He had plenty of ability, passion for a good cause, and considerable gifts which he could use if he was so inclined. He

9

just lacked self-discipline. His time of restraint with us made it clear that he was no alcoholic. Drink for him was just an escape from reality. By now Will was too overwhelmed by his own feelings to make any further reply, and the rest of our walk was spent in thoughtful silence.

*   *   *

A sunny day was followed by a lovely evening. There was no moon but a prolonged afterglow, and the air was rich with the scent of meadowsweet and honeysuckle. Will decided to breathe in the wine of kings, the unpolluted air of Ashenridge.

"Just don't mix it with the deadly odours from the brewer's barrel," Mary called out to him. Her voice sounded lighthearted enough, but I knew she was giving Will a strong message.

"Never fear. Trust honest William," he said in parting.

The rich heady scents of summer filled his lungs; flowers, harvest, and malted barley. Strong, enticing, powerful. After all, what could be more pleasant after a good stroll than to slip into the Coach and Horses for a quick drink on the way home?

It was a quiet night at the inn. Just a few locals sitting round the bar. Will soon found himself the life and soul of the party. Here was a fresh audience for all his stories. Up shot his arms, on went the grand theatrical voice, and out came the tale of the barmaid and the bishop, the actress and the Prince of Wales. When the locals discovered he was Mary's cousin he was plied with even more drinks. At some stage he became aware of Glentie Moore flirting with him and at closing time they ambled out arm in arm. The locals loved it.

I was aware of none of this, but finding Will still out at bedtime I strolled down to the inn. It was closed and there was neither sight nor sound of him. Assuming he was simply on a longer walk than we expected, Mary and I got into bed and were soon fast asleep.

I got up early the next morning. The postman had already been, but what really attracted my attention was something on the hall table, something green and yellow. Before my eyes lay a large bunch of what had once been the most magnificent of dahlias. Now they were a crushed and sorry sight, and beside them was a note. "I'm sorry. Will."

Will's room was empty. He was gone. Gone, too, from their bed in our garden were the very best of Reg's prize dahlias. I raced from room to room with the ill-fated flowers and Will's note still in my hand. Could there be some way of saving the situation? Hearing the noise, Mary came out of the bedroom still in her dressing gown. She took one look at the note, shrugged her shoulders, snatched the flowers from my hand and threw the lot into the garden.

The front door sounded as if it were being attacked by a battering ram. Not even a legion of angels could have calmed the red-faced Reg Pert who ranted on our doorstep, his fists clenched in rage. Without waiting for an explanation from me he poured out his wrath. Eventually he paused to recover his breath and I tried to tell him how our visitor had accidentally picked the wrong flowers thinking they were Mary's.

"Haccidentally!" he bellowed back at me. "That drunken sot you calls your relation. You gets 'im 'alf drunk and then sends 'im down the Coach and 'orses tellin' they filthy tales. 'Tis just like you drunken passons. A disgrace you be, a b . . . disgrace. I tells you this, 'twill be the last time you sees me in this garden. After all I've done. B . . . passons!" And with that he marched off.

As soon as Mary had collected her thoughts and got dressed, she rang the secretary of the flower show to explain what had happened. Naturally she intended to withdraw her exhibits. The secretary was most sympathetic but would have none of it. Every entry was needed to make the show worthwhile. Reluctantly Mary agreed to enter her flowers.

That Saturday afternoon is one I will never forget. Not only did I get angry looks, but some people I knew well seemed strangely preoccupied. Annie Cook was apparently too busy gazing at the prize Windsor beans to notice me. Even Len Cooksley, my good-natured sexton, only gave a quick nod as he hurried to the tea-tent. Today he was resplendent in a brown sports jacket with huge checks.

I remembered seeing it at a recent jumble sale. He could never resist a good bargain and normally would have delighted in telling me all about it.

To crown it all, Mary won the dahlia cup that should by rights have been Reg's. She rose to the occasion by saying she would neither accept it nor allow her name to be engraved on it. She insisted that, due to some very unfortunate circumstances, the person who really ought to have won had been prevented from exhibiting. This brought praise and clapping from the crowd. Once Mary had pricked the bubble the tension eased and people were no longer embarrassed to talk about what had happened.

Reg never came to our garden again, nor did he forgive us for what had happened. A day or two later I learnt that the person who'd pressed more and more drinks on Will the night before the flower show was none other than Reg Pert himself!

Chapter 3

Nobody's Poodle

My early days at Ashenridge were marked by a number of crises. In the case of the flower show, at least Mary was able to bring some good out of what had happened. Ten months before that an event took place which at the time looked a total disaster. It was when I paid my very first visit to Ashenridge that I nearly made the biggest mistake of my life.

I remember how I'd hesitated on Colonel Water's doorstep. So much depended on what happened next. The knocker was heavy. It positively shone from a fresh coat of black paint and I tested it gingerly with my finger before lifting it. Even then I still hesitated. I held the knocker in my hand and noticed the only thing not painted on the door was the spur of metal it struck. This had been worn down over the years, but had anyone ever given that door a more crucial knock than the one I was about to deliver?

It was October 1956. That morning the bright autumn sun seemed to shine encouragingly upon me, but there were dark clouds in the distance. Its rays also lit up the roses still flowering round the porch of the Colonel's thatched cottage. He was one of the four church-wardens I had travelled so far to see, hopefully to become their new rector. The bishop of Whiteminster had told me that Colonel Waters was very much the leading spokesman amongst them. I knew this first visit would be of prime importance. I must get it right. If he liked me, then I had a fair chance of my wishes being fulfilled.

The next minute I found myself face to face with a solid sixty-five-year-old man with a fine crop of silver hair. He eyed me for a moment as if inspecting one of his troops prior to some campaign. Then looking with dismay at the young man who stood before him, he said, "I must confess I was expecting a much older man."

Before I had a chance to say anything, he continued, "You see, we don't want any changes here at Ashenridge. We like things just the way they are."

After coffee the Colonel led me round his extensive garden. "Yes, we want things to stay as they are. Everything straight from the Prayer Book. None of that high church nonsense here. We expect services at 8.00, 11.00 and 6.30. What's more, we'd object to having some other parish tacked on to us. There's plenty enough to do here, even for a young man like you."

As we climbed the slope at the end of the garden, he paused to recover his breath. In more modified tones he returned to the purpose of my visit. "We want someone who'll be content with the old ways. Someone who'll take services, visit the sick . . . be involved in everything we do in the parish."

*   *   *

This was hardly what I'd expected. Knowing of my wish to work in the countryside, the bishop had told me about the rather run-down parish of Ashenridge. In future it would be combined with its tiny neighbour, Combe Peter. The previous rector of Ashenridge came there forty years ago, full of enthusiasm and ideas. As he aged things gradually went downhill. Mr Weatherspoon, the previous vicar of Combe Peter, had died two years ago while still in office. Uncertainty about the future of that parish meant delaying any appointment. Both churches were struggling to survive at all.

Although they couldn't see it, they really needed a man from a different generation with new ideas. In those days it was not easy to get young, energetic clergy to work in sleepy rural England. I'd therefore expected the churchwarden to be pleased at the prospect of having someone my age and was somewhat surprised at his reaction.

14

The possibility of such a reception had not crossed my mind as, full of excitement, I'd driven that morning deep into the West Country. A weak sun picked out autumn tints on trees and hedgerows. Scarlet apples smiled at me from orchards, and crimson Virginia creeper blazed from old stone buildings. My eyes, however, were looking to the hills ahead, to the kind of countryside in which I grew up on the family farm.

Dressed in my little-used brown suit, I approached these remote hill parishes, glad to leave behind the oppressive atmosphere of Millington, where I'd been curate for three years. I was glad to get away from the clerical black which people expected me to wear; away from the restrictive atmosphere of a large town, so alien to my upbringing; away from the anonymity of urban life. If I came to a place like this I could be myself – country born, country thinking, country through and through.

"You're a fool," persisted my dark-suited contemporaries. "You'll be wasted in the countryside, buried there forever."

I knew only too well that country parishes were perceived as places where elderly clergy went to work before retiring. But things were changing fast in rural areas. No longer could the Church of England afford to place one man in every small parish. There was neither the money nor the manpower. In future, more and more parishes would be brought together. Telephones and unrationed petrol were transforming country life. Challenging work lay ahead for a new generation of younger clergy. I was keen to be a part of it.

*   *   *

After a substantial lunch with Colonel and Mrs Waters, it was time to meet Fred Eastridge, the other churchwarden. He glared at me and, rather reluctantly, showed me round a tired-looking Ashenridge Church. His ruddy complexion and pronounced nose made him look like a cross cockatoo. To add to this impression, his ruffled-up hair resembled a crest.

Eyeing my youthful figure with obvious disapproval, he announced, "When Mr Turner was 'ere," and went on to speak of days gone by when everything was perfect. How the adoring parishioners packed the church for his farewell occasion. All his services were good and his sermons short. What was more, he called on everyone regularly. He went to great pains to distribute small sums of charity money to old people at Christmas and Easter. He chaired all manner of local meetings, and set up or revived the Sunday School, choir, youth club, and drama society, to name but a few of his achievements. Apparently he thought nothing of getting up in the early hours of the morning to make sure the church stove was still burning. His virtues were never-ending. He took a particular pride in polishing brass, arranged flowers, and would never let anyone else put up the altar hangings in case the colours were incorrect for the Sunday in question.

Country clergy lending a hand with practical tasks is right and normal, but I got the impression Mr Turner hadn't been too good at delegating. He seemed to have filled his days doing tasks others could have done equally well. I felt I needed to make this point right from the start, so I asked Fred whether he felt that in future the parishioners might like to share some of these jobs. Staring at me in horror he retorted, "That's what you'm paid for."

Edging away from the suspicious eye of Fred, my hopes of seeing the church alone were soon dashed. Oiling the hinges of the vestry door was a small, dark-haired man in grey trousers and a dark-blue jacket, which I guessed were the remains of his 'demob' suit.

"Afternoon, sir, I'm Len Cooksley, the sexton. I 'spect you'm wonderin' what I'm doin' with this 'inge. Well, 'tis like this." Off he went into a rapidly spoken and complicated explanation. After a little while I became aware that he kept referring to 'they lastics' and something about 'closin' it'. Assuming he'd found the remedy for the groaning hinge by using elastic, I chipped in. "Yes, I'm sure that's the best solution."

My remark seemed to kill off any further conversation. He gave me a sideways look, and after an alarmed "Do 'e think so, sir?" left me on my own. What on earth had I done to upset him?

Months later I discovered that Len was notorious for getting his words muddled. By "they lastics" he'd meant the Church Commissioners. Formerly called the Ecclesiastical Commissioners, that was how he still thought of them and simplified a rather complicated word into "lastics". So, not only had my comment silenced him, but my apparent desire to see churches closed went round like wildfire and helped to create a very hostile atmosphere later that day.

*   *   *

My next shock was the rectory. Passing the remains of an entrance gate now lying amongst overgrown laurel bushes, we entered the grounds of a very neglected house. As we struggled along the drive, knee-deep in brambles, Fred Eastridge spoke of all the happy events which had taken place in the garden 'in Mr Turner's time'.

Fred seemed quite oblivious to the appalling state of this large nineteenth-century house. Slates were missing from the roof, weeds grew out of leaking gutters and the rotting timbers appeared not to have been painted since the reign of Queen Victoria.

The interior bore remnants of heavy Edwardian wallpaper and dark paint. So decayed was the dining room floor that Fred nearly fell through it into the cellar. Dismissing this as nothing, he showed me the kitchen with its rusty cracked cooking range. In the scullery beyond there was an enormous hand pump. On the end of its handle was a lump of lead about the size of a cannon ball. I was assured it only took five hundred pumps a day to fill the tank in the roof. This then supplied water to all the taps in the house. One or two rooms actually had electric lights in them!

Mary should have been with me on this visit, but a bout of 'flu meant she'd had to stay in bed. I was glad she wasn't with me. She'd have been horrified.

Yet another blow came when I spotted an old man in corduroys and cloth cap emerging from the overgrown vegetable garden. This was

17

the ill-fated Reg Pert. By the way he spoke he made it clear that he'd played the part of fairy godfather to Mr Turner, having the free use of the garden in exchange for keeping down the weeds. So, just like the Colonel, Reg was also hoping for another elderly incumbent. He wanted to be left alone in his two-acre jungle.

*   *   *

The programme for my visit had been planned with military precision by the Colonel. Coffee at eleven o'clock, interview until lunch, walkabout with Fred followed by tea, then a brief meeting with one or two selected church officials before my departure.

"I wouldn't waste time with them, they're just an afterthought," said the Colonel when I discovered that Combe Peter appeared nowhere on his schedule.

"In any case," he added, "the others are coming at four o'clock. That means you'll be able to leave for home before it gets dark."

By now I didn't care whether or not I offended anyone. I felt very sorry for the other parish, tiny though it might be. So I made it clear that, if it was to become part of my care, Combe Peter should have a fair crack of the whip. I stressed that the bishop required me to see both parishes and asked for the meeting to be retimed. I also made it clear that representatives from both parishes must be present. It was time the Colonel realised I was thirty-six, not just a boy straight from school. If I were to come here, I would make the decisions. I was going to be nobody's poodle!

*   *   *

It was only a short drive along the ridge road to Combe Peter. Within minutes the River Badger came into view with the moors in the distance. Pausing to take in the autumn air, I could see far behind me the market town of Leighford which lay astride the river. A cloud of migrating starlings passed overhead. After a while the high hedge banks along the narrow road opened out, the lane widened and the

18

verges became wet and rushy. A signpost directed me to the right and I found myself dipping down into the tiny hamlet of Combe Peter.

Of the two churchwardens only Steve Birchall could be found. He apologised that Mr Hammerford was away from his farm that day. I was surprised that he didn't seem offended at having had no prior notice of my visit.

Far from sitting back in his retirement, Steve Birchall devoted all his energies to growing soft fruit in the two south-facing fields adjacent to his bungalow. Soon he and his wife, Rita, were telling me about the well-attended church they used to go to in suburbia. How different things were in Combe Peter. Hardly anyone went to church. The organist was slow, they sang old-fashioned hymns and kept slavishly to the Prayer Book. The Sunday School was a local joke.

I asked how they'd managed in the two years since Mr Weatherspoon died. Steve was evasive, but Rita rescued him by explaining that a retired clergyman had been coming fortnightly. To justify his own irregular attendance, Steve explained how he hated sermons. Why couldn't they have two-way discussion between the man in the pulpit and those in the pews? He could tell I was a progressive sort of chap. Surely this was the sort of thing I would like?

The Victorian church I was shown round was depressing. Built on the site of a much older church, nothing of the former building survived. It confirmed everything the Birchalls told me. A few tatty service books, mould creeping over a shabby harmonium and moths making a feast of the hangings. Most of the mantles in the gas lamps were broken or missing, and the vicar's stall was riddled with woodworm.

A year ago the Archdeacon had suggested closing the church. Most people were indignant about it, but Steve thought it a good idea. Being an ex-serviceman and keen to support British Legion projects for the war wounded, he said he would have loved to convert the building into a workshop for the disabled.

*   *   *

Tired and frustrated I entered the final phase of the day. Ten people were waiting impatiently in the Colonel's drawing-room. I'm afraid they were going to get a piece of my mind.

Colonel Waters gave a brief introduction, then reiterated all the things people would expect of me, which could simply be summed up by saying they wanted a second Mr Turner. He then asked if there were any points I wished to make. I took a deep breath, said a silent prayer, and waded in.

"I've been trying to make a mental list of all the things you would expect me to do if I were to come here. You seem to require a brilliant conductor of services, a health visitor, businessman, flower arranger, boilerman and brass cleaner, to name but a few. Indeed, people seem to be under the impression that I'm paid to do every single one of those jobs.

Do you think this is what Jesus envisaged when he sent his disciples out two by two to proclaim his kingdom? Did he intend that his followers should simply look on from the pews, perhaps patting the parson on the back if he did well, or grumbling if one Sunday morning he'd forgotten to polish the candlesticks?"

A glance round the room showed that some were quite enjoying this, but not Fred Eastridge. Encouraged, I continued. "I'm not a lazy man. I'm used to hard work. For years I worked on my father's farm. I served in the Royal Army Medical Corps in the war. After demobilisation I married a clergyman's daughter. Then, with difficulty, I adjusted to academic work at a theological college, which was rather like going back to school. For the last three years I've been a curate at Millington working morning, noon and night, all on a stipend many would regard as laughable. During all that time I've never once been asked to arrange flowers or stoke the church boiler.

If I were to come here, I would be the rector of Ashenridge *and* Combe Peter. More and more the Church of England is being forced to put parishes together. We cannot look backwards. The clergy and the congregations of the future must share the work more and more, otherwise they'll never cope with all the changes that are bound to come."

The temperature was going up in the room. "Twice the pay for 'alf the work," came the voice of a latecomer. The speaker was another cross-looking cockatoo, a younger version of Fred Eastridge. I remembered being told that Fred was driven round by his son, Peter. As he sat there blowing out his cheeks, one or two grinned at his remark, but I was annoyed.

"I don't believe in change for change's sake, but change there must be. Look how tractors and milking machines have taken over on your farms and electric power in your homes. Think of the cars, wirelesses and refrigerators. They make life easier for so many people. Yet in a rapidly changing world you expect the church to remain entirely unchanged."

"It isn't the same thing at all," someone muttered.

"Fine countrymen 'e is. Be closin' all our churches 'afore us knows what," came another choice remark.

I'd overstepped the mark and turned everyone against me, or so it seemed. I felt like Alice in Wonderland when the whole pack of cards rose up against her. I quickly thanked my hosts for their kindness and the others for sparing me their time, and left.

*   *   *

Angry, deflated, too tired to think properly, I drove home. If ever I was to be offered another of his country parishes I had to get word to the bishop before he heard from Ashenridge. I wrote him the letter I'd rehearsed on my homeward journey, then having posted it went upstairs. Mary was still feeling a bit under the weather and my news didn't help. She sat up in bed and suddenly became very angry. "Oh Jack, how could you. Have you forgotten how my father moved into a house that was completely run down, but the diocese did a wonderful job on it. As for the churchwardens, why, all country wardens are the same. You should have known that and not made such a fool of yourself."

Between her sobs she told me in no uncertain terms she would have loved the rectory garden. Paul was increasingly interested in nature and Ann loved everything to do with wildlife. Now, without consulting anyone, our chance of living in the countryside was ruined. After my stupid behaviour no bishop would ever offer me anything like it again.

As Mary spoke, the horror of what I'd done came home to me. I'd probably condemned myself to a world of grey suits, people in nine-to-five jobs, and an urban life of which I had little understanding or real sympathy. I'd turned my back on all those rich country characters I loved and, worst of all, denied my family the chance of living in a part of the country many people would envy.

*   *   *

A week later two letters arrived. The first was a curt message from the bishop. He thanked me for my letter but felt it would be difficult to offer me any other rural parish as it appeared I could not rise to the challenge such places were bound to present. However, on the strength of a letter from one of the churchwardens at Ashenridge he thought I might want to reconsider my decision.

The other letter, equally brief, came from Colonel Waters. It read, "You're quite right. I admire your courage and honesty. We very much hope you will be our rector."

*   *   *

In the closing days of October 1956 three major events took place. The Hungarians rose up against their Communist masters, the British marched into Suez, and in my own small world I wrote a letter to the bishop saying I would, after all, like him to offer me the parishes of Ashenridge and Combe Peter.

That same day Mary went out and bought Wellington boots for all the family.

Chapter 4

Sport Up At The Hall

I'd only been working a few weeks in my new parishes. The rectory was still in chaos with workmen everywhere and the family camped in one or two rooms. Yet already I was facing my first crisis. Ashenridge Church Annual Meeting was about to test all the faith and skill I possessed.

"There'll be sport up at the hall this evening," commented Jim Stillman as he looked out of the door of the Coach and Horses, Ashenridge's only pub. Then, shaking his bald head and stroking his chin in a superior sort of way, he added, "For what it's worth."

To Jim, Ashenridge Church and all it stood for seemed like a quaint survival from another age. There it stood in the heart of the village, its bells waking him earlier than he would have chosen on a Sunday morning. He regarded with mild tolerance the simple people who attended the services. Pleasant though he was to me, he considered clergy to be gullible fools muttering mumbo-jumbo over brides and babies, or uttering sweet sentiments over the departed as they were sent on their way to a make-believe world. Little did he realise that among the congregation were some whose faith had been sorely tested through the horrors of war, depression, sickness or disability.

No matter what Jim thought about the church, that evening people were pouring into Ashenridge Parish Hall from all directions.

"'Tis like the Christmas Whist Drive all over again," Len Cooksley said as he helped arrange more seats at the back of the hall.

The car park was full, the village street was lined with vehicles.

No one could remember so many people coming to the Annual Meeting before. The election of churchwardens usually passed by almost unnoticed, but this year was different. Old Fred Eastridge had collapsed and died in the middle of lambing. Thirty years earlier he had taken over from his father as people's warden. Now Fred's son, Peter, assumed he would succeed his father. It took me a long time to convince him that nowadays in the Church of England things do not work quite like that. He would need to be elected by the parishioners, yes the whole parish, not just the regular churchgoers.

As he arrived at the hall that evening, Peter eyed me with a look of contempt. I had already tried to explain everything to him as gently as I could. Sadly, I think he misread my smile and thought I was mocking him. Influenced by his father's views, he considered me a lazy and selfish man. Far more money than he could earn in one year was being spent on the rectory. By taking on more than one parish he assumed I would be paid extra but do less and less in Ashenridge.

"Father said us needs to keep an eye on you. 'E knowed you wanted to 'ave less Sunday services and stop they old folk 'aving their 'alf-crown charity on Maundy Thursday, and . . ."

A glare from Jane, his wife, stopped him. She seemed to be a very gentle woman, but the lines on her face suggested she did not find life easy. Remembering he was actually trying to win my support, he modified his angry tone and we were soon on safer subjects like how to raise money for church funds.

If Peter had attended church regularly there wouldn't have been a problem. He insisted to his friends that he was 'church', meaning he came to services about twice a year. He felt this was quite enough. The law did not require him to be a weekly churchgoer, so why should the rector? After all, he led just as good a life as his neighbours, and what was more he'd been born here.

Peter's anger backfired in two ways. Thanks to the fuss he made people realised for the first time the vestry meeting was no mere formality. There really would be an election at which they could choose the next churchwarden. Furthermore, Peter was known to be difficult, and his hostility towards me did not wholly commend him to the parish. It also happened that there was another possible candidate, Will Swift.

Will had attended agricultural college. He left home a Christmas and Harvest churchgoer and returned at the end of his training a dedicated Anglican who rarely missed a service. What was more, since settling back in Ashenridge he was always available when needed. One day he'd be seen on the church roof nailing slates back after a storm. On another occasion he might be clearing gutters or sweeping paths. Shortly before the service which marked my start here, Will had polished all the pews in the church and linseed oiled the screen and doors. What a difference it made. The building now felt fresh and cared for, something that had been lacking when Fred Eastridge had shown me round the previous autumn.

When I arrived at the hall that evening Will was busy working with Len Cooksley putting out the old benches. The newer, more comfortable folding chairs were already fully occupied.

Looking round I could spot the regular churchgoers. They were not alone in wanting Will to be their churchwarden. Having seen him in action round the church, I felt many of the newcomers might also vote for him. The remainder of the crowd were, for the most part, long-standing locals on whom Peter was counting for support.

As 7.30pm approached, Colonel Waters glanced at his watch. It was time to get started. We began the proceedings with one minute's silence in memory of Fred Eastridge. After a prayer I welcomed everyone to the vestry meeting, saying how good it was that the parishioners showed so much interest in their church and how I hoped this would be a sign of things to come.

I began safely enough with words of appreciation.

"Mr Eastridge was a great son of Ashenridge, a noted farmer, a traditionalist who loved his church dearly." Peter glowed with satisfaction at my eulogy, but even so he kept looking round. There were rather a lot of people in the hall who were strangers to him. Not a good sign.

No doubt Peter would have been pleased had I concluded by saying how splendid it would be if the Eastridge tradition were to continue.

Instead I turned to Colonel Waters and expressed my warm appreciation for a man I had come to like and respect. I thanked him for his great help to me in my new parish and commended not only his forthrightness, but also his willingness to listen to the other point of view. Some people smiled at this recalling my first encounter with him.

It was then my privilege to nominate Colonel Waters as rector's warden for the coming year. A look of approval passed round the room.

Next I came to the matter of people's warden. I invited nominations, making it clear that if more than one name was received there would have to be an election.

Like a shot, Peter Eastridge's unmarried sister, Sarah, got up and proposed her brother. At my request for a seconder half a dozen people put up their hands.

"Are there any other nominations?" I asked. There was a pause. Then a lady wearing a large hat more suited to a garden party than the parish hall stood up and announced in a loud fruity voice, "I would like to nominate Mr Will Swift."

Mrs Batchelor was hardly the ideal person to propose Will. She was still regarded as a newcomer to the village. A few years ago she'd moved into a large house adjoining the churchyard and since her retirement had adopted the church as one of her main interests. For all her good intentions she had a knack of never getting things quite right.

I asked for a seconder. An awkward pause followed. Eventually the organist put up his hand. With no other nominations, voting commenced. Colonel Waters was let out of declaring himself by being appointed teller. First I asked for hands in favour of Mr Eastridge. A good half the room supported him. The Colonel and I counted and wrote down a number. Then I asked for hands in favour of Mr Swift. A few were raised. Then, as people started looking round at their neighbours, more and more hands went up. The Colonel and I did another count. Again he wrote down a figure. When we counted the people in the room it became clear a lot of them had voted twice.

We therefore resorted to a secret ballot. Just to make sure there was no doubt about the result, I took up the Colonel's suggestion that the two proposers check the counting. When we were all satisfied I declared the result. Peter Eastridge 47 votes . . . Will Swift 51. Peter looked as black as thunder, gave me a threatening scowl and stormed out of the hall, closely followed by his sister and a few friends.

The rest of the evening was taken up with the Annual Meeting which, to everyone's relief, turned out to be uneventful and quite lighthearted.

It was back to normal in the Church of England.

Chapter 5

It Couldn't Happen To Someone Like You

On the Monday morning after the flower show I had an appointment to visit a local farm to arrange the baptism of baby Margaret Broadford. Mrs Broadford senior met me at the back door. She was a slight woman with tightly permed greying hair. Her mouth was pinched and she spoke in a shrill voice. After a few words and with a scream loud enough to waken the dead, she summoned Sandra, her daughter-in-law.

I felt very sorry for Sandra. The original idea had been for her and Trevor, her husband, to move into a bungalow which they intended to build at the end of the farm lane. Every time they applied for planning permission, it was turned down by the District Council on some technical point. In the end they simply contented themselves with living in part of the old farmhouse. The young couple did have a kitchen of their own, but no separate entrance. I wondered how much chance Sandra was getting to set up her own home.

"Sorry us kept you waitin', Mr Longfield," said Sandra. "You must be a busy man." She smiled at me, her friendly brown eyes peering under her fair curly hair. "Us's been busy puttin' baby right." Then she added: "There now, where's that Christenin' form to?" After another "Sorry" she disappeared once more into the depths of the house.

"'Er's been messin' 'bout with that little maid for over an hour now. Us can't think why 'er takes so long." Mrs Broadford sounded unsympathetic.

Sandra reappeared carrying baby Margaret and the form.

"I always like to meet the couple together before a baptism so I can explain exactly what we are doing. When can I find you and Trevor in?"

For a brief moment Sandra's face fell. Meanwhile Mrs Broadford went out of the room to find the family diary.

"How about Wednesday evening?" I asked.

"Sorry, not then. Not in the evenin'," came Sandra's reply. After lunch was not suitable either. Eventually we settled on eleven o'clock the following Wednesday.

As I crawled back home behind a large cattle feed lorry it occurred to me that, despite all her 'sorries', Sandra seemed content to live under Mrs Broadford's wing, but I sensed all was not well. Perhaps the answer lay with the elusive Trevor. Sandra had certainly made enough excuses to delay my meeting him. I hoped next Wednesday might throw some light on things.

*   *   *

I was beginning to realise that Ashenridge was a bit of an uphill task. As a curate in a large church all the little jobs had been carried out by other people. When the first vicar left I took on more responsibilities for a while, but even so many things still looked after themselves. Now I was truly glad to be back in the real countryside which was my home. My critics had been wrong. I found my work here truly fulfilling, and thanks to my farming background I had a fair understanding of country folk, which many town clergymen take years to learn. There was, however, a price to pay. No sooner had I arrived than several people came up to me and said "Now you're here I can hand this over to you."

Despite my declared intention before I came to Ashenridge, I found myself taking on all manner of jobs. Soon I was running the Sunday School and auditing the WI accounts. I held the parish hall key, became master of ceremonies at parish parties, and secretary, chairman or treasurer of any number of organisations. In moderation it might not have mattered, but the list grew and grew and it became less and less easy to say 'No'.

*   *   *

On the Wednesday, Sandra herself was waiting for me by the back door. She was sorry that mother was out, she'd taken baby Margaret for a walk in the pram, and would I mind coming into their sitting room?

As I went through the kitchen Mr Broadford senior was sitting at the huge table, a beef sandwich in one hand, a mug of tea in the other. He was a large, genial man, and as I went past he shrugged his shoulders and gave me a cheerful smile. His look said it all.

A tour through several rooms in this old longhouse eventually led us to Sandra and Trevor's own quarters. Here I was hastily led past a little-used front hall, cluttered with numerous boxes, all covered with a sheet.

"Sorry, Trevor isn't in yet," Sandra said. "He'll be in drekley."

After five minutes or so Trevor appeared, scrubbed down, ready for inspection. With a "Mornin' Mr Longfield", he sat down, leaving us to do the talking. He seemed about as pleased to see me as a thunderstorm during hay making. He was of slight build but lacked the wiriness of his mother. He appeared pale and tired. In fact he reminded me of the rather weakly onions our son Paul had produced on his first attempt at vegetable growing. He looked as if putting one milk churn on the stand at the end of their lane would be enough to finish him off!

I made several unsuccessful attempts to draw him into the conversation. Even a few warning signals flashing in his direction from Sandra achieved nothing. In the end I waded into the things I would normally say about baptism. I explained that this service is about the eternal destiny of the child, not a mere naming ceremony. It really only makes sense when both parents bring their children to church and come regularly themselves. Sandra was listening carefully; Trevor was nearly asleep. From time to time he stirred and nodded in agreement with whatever I said. It was obvious that using this line of

30

least resistance was how he coped with his mother and Sandra. There seemed to be no spark of life in him.

I thought a change of subject would help. "So when Margaret gets a bit older, I expect she'll have her own room?"

"Well 'tisn't as easy as that," Sandra explained. "Us only 'as a very small part of the 'ouse. Us could do with a bit more, only mother can't spare us any more rooms see."

She explained that their latest application to build a bungalow was turned down because the access to the lane was too narrow.

"Well, if it's only an access problem couldn't you remove some of the hedge and apply again?" I mentioned something similar when my parents took over grandfather's farm.

"I don't rightly know," replied Trevor, for the first time becoming interested in the conversation.

"Trouble is 'e's too darn lazy," broke in Sandra. "Won't bother to fill in more of they forms. Won't do nort 'bout that hedge near the entrance. Too many roots to pull out," she said, referring to some huge tree stumps in the bank. Then, turning to Trevor, she added, "If you didn't spend so much time . . ."

Trevor was saved by the bell. "That'll be Jim Stillman," he said, making his escape to deal with a delivery.

"Us'll tell you the truth, rector, 'tis they darned old bottles."

Once Sandra got started nothing would stop her. Trevor could only work in the mornings. Too much to drink at lunch time and he was in no fit state to work in the afternoons and every evening he consumed more! That was what the hall was full of – beer bottles. As she went on I got the picture. Trevor was a weak man, buffeted by his mother and Sandra, henpecked by both. Too withdrawn to go out, once he'd found the right girl at the Young Farmer's Club, he'd just sat at home and drank. What a life!

At that point Trevor joined us again. I detected a look of triumph on his face. It was not hard to guess the story he'd just heard from Jim Stillman.

"They say you 'ad problems on Saturday, rector," he announced, trying to hide a grin.

I've always believed in making the best of a bad situation, so I sailed in. "You've just heard about someone with a drink problem, a member of my family called Will. Am I right?"

Trevor looked embarrassed.

"Well, Trevor, let me tell you something about him. At heart he's a good man. He has lots of charm, he's fun to be with. In the war he did exceptionally dangerous work behind the lines. He could have achieved much in life, but sadly he made some bad decisions and wasted his talents. Drink is just an escape from reality for him. His self-respect has gone. What's more, Trevor, you're doing just the same thing. You have a wonderful wife and baby daughter, you have all the skills to be a first-rate farmer. You must be the envy of many men your age, so make the best of it. You may have problems, but face up to them. Will made the mistake of trying to run away from his."

I waited for the explosion, but instead Trevor was quiet for a minute or two then started to laugh. "Us didn't think it could happen to someone like you. Us allus thought you folks was different with your dog collars and preachin'. Cor, you'm a farmer's son, too!"

*   *   *

A few weeks later the baptism of baby Margaret took place in Ashenridge Church. It was a very special occasion made all the better seeing Sandra and Trevor so happy together.

Outside the church we passed Jim 'for what it's worth' Stillman walking off a good Sunday lunch. I caught a glimpse of him stroking his chin as he watched our procession. He never saw Trevor's broad grin as, later that day, we entered the farm lane where someone had been busy digging out a section of the hedge and old tree stumps.

And he didn't hear Trevor whisper, "Guess what, rector. Us 'ave filled in another of they plannin' forms."

Chapter 6

'Tis Kitty

"I wouldn't go there if I was you," Mrs Trout advised me. "Us never goes there," she continued, shaking her head and pointing with disapproval at a dilapidated cottage lying at an angle behind other houses in the village street. A muddy back lane passed in front of it, becoming a grassy path as it made its way across a field to the church.

"You won't be wanted there," others had warned me.

Mary, with her rectory upbringing, confirmed this opinion. "Quite right. My father would only call when people asked him. He said we had no right interfering with those people who wanted nothing to do with the church."

However, an inner voice reminded me about a Shepherd seeking the lost . . .

One showery Friday in September I happened to be passing the cottage. The garden was a sea of weeds and litter. Long rank grass surrounded a broken armchair. The remnants of a rocking horse peeped out from a bed of overgrown nettles. A doll's pram housed a bed of dandelions, and a few chickens wandered miserably amongst patches of dock, pecking at some disgusting scraps of food.

It was getting dark. An oil lamp in one room shone through a broken window. This wreck of old England with its twisted, undulating ridge of tiles stood out against the red afterglow of a troubled sky. I wondered how much rainwater was seeping into its pathetic hulk. It was reminiscent of country slums of earlier days, walls running green and damp, cracked greasy ceilings blackened with smoke, unwashed children running around in the ragged remains of someone else's cast-off clothes. Ten years of the welfare state had not eliminated every hovel.

"Go to bed yer b . . . little toad," boomed a coarse female voice from within. This was followed by the crash of what sounded like a large piece of crockery. A door slammed. Then all was silent. Out of sight I listened for a few moments, but nothing more happened. It was harvest time, and I was needed in church.

*　　*　　*

In the middle of Ashenridge village, just by the Coach and Horses, stood a wooden bus shelter. It was kept in immaculate order and woe betide any child who dared deface it. Built in the 1930s, it commemorated those who fell in the 1914-18 War. The names of those who died in the Second World War were added later. This building was the outcome of a long dispute. Originally money had been collected to erect a war memorial in the churchyard. Then, in the days when church and chapel were very much divided, the Methodists expressed strong resentment that it should be at the church. In the end everyone settled for a compromise – the bus shelter.

Besides providing cover for those waiting for the daily bus, the shelter was also a very popular meeting place. Teenagers made respectful use of it in the evenings, but in the morning it was the turn of the womenfolk. Day after day the bench inside would be filled with them. Evidently they were well organised, for often they held cups of tea in their hands. I discovered it was Flossie Bluett who produced the tea. Flossie was the widow of the former licensee of the Coach and Horses. She lived in a nearby cottage and on sunny days this morning ritual suited her. She still had difficulty adjusting to life not entertaining people in the pub.

I found it hard to keep a straight face when passing by the shelter. Chatter – chatter – chatter – laugh – laugh – laugh. Then as I went by, silence!

34

"Morning, ladies," I ventured.

"Good morning, Mr Longfield. Isn't it a nice day," or words to that effect would greet me from the assembled company.

"What's the news today?"

Usually there was no news suitable for my ears, except if a baby had been born, or some disaster had struck. Clearly the company of others was not required in the bus shelter so, without delay, I'd go on my way. As soon as I was out of earshot the laughter and chatter would start again.

However, there was a mystery here. Amongst the company, always sitting in a corner, was a shrivelled and bent over little woman with untidy grey hair, a cigarette perpetually hanging from her mouth. If her budget could run to so many cigarettes it fell short of providing her with new clothes. She always wore the same off-white print dress with a weary grey cardigan lodged on her shoulders. One tarnished button held the whole thing together. In my presence she never spoke, but her half-opened mouth showed that a lack of buttons was matched by a lack of teeth and those that did survive were discoloured.

One day I approached the shelter from behind. I got right up to it before being spotted. The conversation stopped immediately, but not before my ears recognised the voice of the woman in the corner. There was no doubt about it, it was the same voice I'd heard in the dilapidated cottage. My attempts to get her to speak again failed. All that came from that weather-worn face was the hint of a smile.

Blow what Mary said. Blow what other people advised. I was determined to settle this once and for all. I was convinced a country clergyman should know all his people, church, chapel or anything else. Looking straight at the lady in question I said, "I think I know everyone else here, but I don't know your name." There was a shocked silence.

"'Tis Kitty, parson," came the mild reply.

"Where do you live?" I continued.

"Why over to Wishwell Cottage," she said, pointing in the direction I expected. "Was yer thinkin' of comin' to see me?"

One of the other women, evidently anxious to protect me from such an ordeal, stepped in. "Now then Kitty, Mr Longfield's got a great deal of work to do. He's seen you here. Isn't that enough?"

By now Kitty was lighting another cigarette.

"No, there's no need to come to my little 'ouse," she said. "Yer allus sees me when I comes out in the mornin' like this to buy me, er, stamps." I was sure she'd just stopped herself from saying 'cigarettes'.

"Then I won't delay you," I said, moving off and wondering just how many letters she planned to post that day!

*   *   *

One Saturday a tiny girl with the sweetest face appeared in our garden. She seemed to have come from nowhere. Paul and Ann were at home and began to play with her. She must have been almost five. She wore odd rubber boots, a faded blue coat and her fair hair was tied back with a bit of tape. When the children got thirsty Mary invited her in with them to have a drink.

"My name's Becky," she announced to everyone, in a voice surprisingly deep and husky for such a little girl. After her third glass of lemonade and a seventh biscuit, she continued, "My Nan's going to a biscuit factory next Saturday to see how they makes them."

Mary began to cotton on. Next Saturday the Mothers' Union members were going to a factory at Whiteminster followed by a visit to nearby Castle Mount.

The little girl continued, "I'd like to go too. I likes biscuits an' castles an' things."

"Who is your Nan?" Mary was intrigued.

This floored Becky for a minute. Could there be anyone in the whole wide world who did not know who her Nan was?

"Everybody calls her Kitty. She's the lady with the funny arm that sits in the bus shelter."

From my previous description, Mary soon put two and two together. At this point she stiffened. Kitty had never been to a Mothers' Union meeting so how could she possibly expect to go on the outing? The bus was already almost full with members. Once in our last parish

36

Mary had got into trouble when, keen to expand the Young Wives group, she invited one or two non-members to their summer outing. She did not want to get caught again.

She was not to know that very occasionally Kitty did attend the Mothers' Union meetings and was an ardent supporter of its jumble sales. As a result, people took pity on her and it was an unwritten rule that she always went on their outings.

Cautiously Mary said, "Becky, are you sure your Nan's coming on the outing? I've never seen her at any of our meetings."

"Oh yes, I'm sure. Can I come too?"

"You'd better go home and see if your Nan really is coming." Then, taking pity on the little girl Mary added, "If she isn't, I'll see if there's room for you, if your Nan doesn't mind."

*   *   *

Mary told me the whole story as we sat down for lunch. Having met Kitty I had a funny feeling something would happen soon. We sat there like people in an air raid shelter waiting for the blitz. Dessert was just about to be served when the bell rang. I winked at Mary and off she went to the front door. The kitchen door was left open so we could hear everything. It was Kitty right enough. Her voice boomed through the house.

"What the b . . . 'ell did yer tell little Becky?" Just because the parson was too grand to visit me or see me poorly ninety-year-old father who had served in Africa long before we were born. Parson didn't even know 'e existed. 'E just listens to gossips. What if Kitty does like 'er smokes? Yer thinks I ain't fit to go on an outin' . . . I can tell yer what I thinks about parsons . . . 'ow many of they 'ave 'ad to scrub and save? They with their big 'ouses and garden parties and polite curtseys in church. What about poor Kitty strugglin' to keep out the rain, and yer 'as two arms. Look at mine!"

It was then that Mary realised Kitty's left arm was hanging at her side, not by choice but because it was completely limp. Mary was about to say something sympathetic, but didn't get the chance.

"No, I don't want none of yer sympathy. I tells yer I'm through with yer Mothers' Union outin's and jumble sales. As for the 'arvest Festival, yer can tell yer 'usband it'll be a long time 'afore 'e sees Kitty there again."

At this point she turned away, charging down the drive at a fast pace, her good arm swinging round like a windmill. As she did so she muttered something about being a member of the Mothers' Union since the branch started in 1935.

It was not hard to understand the strange power Kitty held as the uncrowned queen of the bus shelter. Not surprisingly, several others followed her lead and pulled out of the trip to Whiteminster. Passing Kitty's court in the mornings now proved awkward. My cheery 'good mornings' were met with silence.

A day or two later I needed to call on Flossie Bluett, the tea lady. Embarassed by the whole affair, she assured me Kitty would soon get over it.

That Sunday in church we heard the story of how Elijah the prophet felt hopelessly outnumbered by hostile people. God protected him, and in the end good came, even to his enemies. As the passage was read, Mary and I both felt reassured that one day things would work out well with Kitty.

*   *   *

One dark November evening some weeks later I came home exhausted from a very trying Church Council meeting at Combe Peter. A whole hour was wasted on a heated debate about whether we should give two guineas to the Cathedral Appeal Fund. Instead of a calming cup of coffee when I got home, I found an anxious Flossie Bluett waiting for me, apologising for troubling me at that hour.

Kitty's father was very ill. There were tales about coughing fits and bringing up blood. Little Becky had been round saying "Granfer's a-dyin'." He might already be dead in the house. Kitty refused to allow her friends in, and everyone was afraid she would do nothing about it as she'd fallen out with the doctor. There was also concern about Becky.

I put my coat on and was soon at Wishwell Cottage. A lamp was burning in the downstairs room. A sullen Kitty opened the door. "Yer'd better come in," she said.

The poor old man lay on an iron bedstead in the kitchen-cum-living room. The lamplight picked out his emaciated profile. The horny hands of a man who had been a farm labourer for fifty years now rested quietly on a rough blanket. At first I thought he was dead. Then, hearing a noise, he opened his eyes and motioned me towards him.

"Pray for me," he implored. "I'm dyin'."

He held my hand like the dying soldiers I tended during the war. I was moved by the scene and started to pray. Together we said the Lord's Prayer. I quoted the 23rd Psalm. Still he held my hands, so I prayed again. This time I noticed the affect it was having on Kitty. I asked if she'd called the doctor.

"No good 'avin' 'im," she said. "Last time all 'e did was be rude 'bout the 'ouse."

"Kitty, listen to me. During the war I was in the Royal Army Medical Corps. Your father's almost certainly dying. We must get a doctor."

Grudgingly she agreed and I went away to phone him. When I returned I took in the scene around me. Some foul-smelling stew was bubbling on a cracked stove. The stench of that meal would linger on my clothes for days. Drips of water running down the chimney hissed as they struck hot metal. I became aware of Becky curled up on a tattered sofa, sobbing as she played with a dirty rag doll. Kitty sat by her father, muttering to herself and chain smoking. My offer to take Becky home for the night was refused.

Two hours later it was over. The doctor had done what he could and the undertaker's work was complete. All was still except for the sound of rain dripping somewhere in the house. Becky had at last fallen asleep. Kitty was slumped over the table, three empty stout bottles in front of her. Few words passed between us and soon she fell into a deep asleep. I crept away from Wishwell Cottage with a heavy heart.

Granfer was buried to the tune of 'Abide with Me' and Psalm 23. When I called on Kitty the day after the funeral she thanked me for staying so long the night the old man died. Then she began to pour out her story.

Wishwell Cottage had been left to Granfer when the old farmer he worked for died. Not a penny had been spent on it and she was too ashamed to invite anyone in. That was why she used the bus shelter. Her husband had died of typhoid years ago and her daughter, Becky's mother, had run off with a lorry driver. Nobody knew who Becky's father was. Tearfully she told me that she only had Becky to live for, and how could she possibly keep her in such a house? Now the doctor had seen it, that would be the end. The 'cruelty man' would come along and take Becky into care.

Kitty was right in her fears about Becky. I warned her she would have a fight on her hands, especially as next term the little girl started school. If Kitty put all she could into improving herself and her home, she might be in with a chance.

Six months later Kitty was allocated one of the new council houses that had just been built at the other end of the village. I was the only person she let go to the old house to help with the move.

Once Kitty got over the idea it was wrong to buy new clothes when there were jumble sales she and Becky began to look smarter. They smelt sweeter, too, after Kitty realised the bath in her new home was not simply a place for storing coal. She even used some of the money raised from the sale of Wishwell Cottage to buy new furniture.

But no one could persuade her to go to the dentist!

Chapter 7

Fifty-Seven, Not Out

"It's doin' more 'arm than good and that's a fact," boomed Mrs Emma Hammerford as she bore down on me at Combe Peter Church's Annual Meeting. "Do you know that only a week or two ago our poor little Tommy needed to make an urgent call after his Sunday dinner, and 'er wouldn't let 'im. Instead 'e 'ad to do it in a corner of the room where 'er'd put 'im."

"Then there was my poor little niece, Fanny," piped up Mrs Small. "I hate to criticise, but she was told off for crying. When she got home they discovered she'd been stung on the hand by a wasp and nothing had been done about it."

"Did nobody tell Miss Kitson about it?" I asked.

"Oh yes," Mrs Small replied. "She was very sorry when she heard what had happened. She came and saw Fanny afterwards and gave her a great big lollypop."

Mrs Hammerford continued her attack. "I'll allow that when 'er knowed what 'er'd done 'er was sorry. 'Er did the same with Tommy, but that iddn' the point. The poor little kids, they'm bored stiff with all they prayers they 'ave to learn by 'eart. What's more 'er tries to make they sing along with that flat voice of 'ers. They say 'tis pandemonium on a Sunday afternoon. A few weeks ago they were all fighting while 'er shut 'er eyes to pray. By the time 'er'd opened them, three 'ad run away. 'Er's too old for the job. You'll 'ave to ask 'er to resign, rector."

Miss Alice Kitson was unwell on the day of this meeting, so it was only in her absence that the complaints were made about her Sunday School. Such an outburst took me by surprise.

*   *   *

My first year's ministry at Combe Peter had witnessed many improvements. Steve Birchall, the churchwarden, abandoned any ideas of converting the church into a workshop for the disabled and he and his wife had become regular worshippers.

His enthusiasm encouraged others to come, and almost imperceptibly more changes followed. New hymns were sung with such gusto that even the organist was forced to quicken her pace. Two or three days of voluntary work not only transformed the church and churchyard but also brought one or two irregulars back to their pews. There were plans to raise funds for new hangings and service books, and even install electric lighting. Joe Hammond, the other churchwarden, had to admit this was becoming more than a nine day wonder.

Nearly every child in the parish attended the Sunday School which Alice Kitson had run for the last fifty-seven years. She was tremendously proud of this and often boasted: "I never missed a Sunday except during the 1947 blizzard."

*   *   *

I knew that Alice liked to go to the church to pray privately. I'd often seen her bird-like figure kneeling in one of the pews, her hands pointing towards heaven. Her's was a strong faith, borne of past trials and suffering which revealed itself in the way she lived. There was a real warmth behind her gentle smile. She took a kindly interest in everyone and would do anything to help if it was needed.

I also knew that her father, the village carpenter, had died of pneumonia when she was very young. Thomas Hayforth then became her step-father, but he found it hard to love a child who was not of his flesh and blood. Frederick and Jane were born of this second marriage, but Alice got little thanks from Thomas Hayforth for all she tried to do as an older sister.

Escape came for Alice when, at fourteen, she went into service at a big house near Taunton. It was her only taste of the outside world. Within a year her step-father had been killed in a railway accident and she returned home. Life for Alice then consisted of looking after her half-brother and half-sister, and later nursing her mother over a long period of failing health.

*   *   *

By the end of the meeting a pretty clear picture had emerged as to what happened at three o'clock on a Sunday afternoon in Combe Peter Church. Sometimes, for a change, Alice asked the children to sing. She was not musical, and as no one could be found to play the ancient harmonium she led in a loud, flat voice. 'Gentle Jesus, Meek and Mild', 'Praise Him, Praise Him All Ye Little Children' and 'Now the Day Is Over'. These were her favourites, and at Christmas 'Away In a Manger' would also be included.

Once she'd started singing she couldn't tell what sort of noise the children were making, and being a little deaf she had no idea whether they were joining in or standing on their heads.

After scolding any children for not knowing their memory pieces, Alice would read them a story from a well-worn book called 'Bible Stories Told to Children'. Then the pupils would be sent home after singing 'Now the Day Is Over'.

While Mrs Small and others were describing this, I looked round the church room. The only teaching aids to be seen were four battered prayer books and a shabby Bible resting on the harmonium.

I was brought back to reality by Emma Hammerford who persisted that Alice should resign. Others nodded in support. Bill Rogers pointed out that, when he was young, thirty five children attended Sunday School, now it was only ten. I asked how many primary school children went on the school bus these days. The answer was twelve.

The figure spoke for itself and enabled me to change the subject without any undertaking to get rid of Alice.

*   *   *

That night I mulled things over. I knew something must be done. I simply could not get Alice out of my mind. She did not need to teach the faith, she was 'the faith' herself. Christianity is more than just learning facts; it's caught rather than taught. Her teaching methods may have been a disaster and I could try to help her there, but I could never bring myself to sack her. I knew I must go and talk to Alice the next day.

As I drove to Combe Peter I still didn't know what I was going to say, and offered up a prayer for God's guidance. Alice's little cottage was one of a small cluster of houses near to the church. Smoke from the chimney told me Alice was at home and her usual welcoming smile greeted me as she opened the door.

As Alice went off to make a cup of tea I gazed round the room. Family photos and prints of rustic scenes decorated the walls. 'Bible Stories Told to Children' rested on top of a cupboard. Nearby was a well-worn Bible, packed with little notes written on thin pieces of paper. Deep down I sensed a peace in that house not a legion of naughty children could destroy. And I sensed a spirituality deeper than mine or that of the entire church council. I knew I need not worry.

"I'm so glad you called in, Mr Longfield," she said, placing a cup in my hand. "You see, I'm concerned about the Sunday School." My heart leapt then fell again as she continued. "No, don't worry, I don't want to give it up, but I am finding it a bit of a strain every week, especially in the winter months."

As nobody in the parish was willing to help, we agreed that after Harvest we'd have a fortnightly family service then she could hold Sunday School on the alternate weeks. Meanwhile I was sure Mary would help her until the August break. Alice seemed pleased with this, although when I offered her a box of crayons and a pile of paper she made it quite clear she did not regard them as suitable teaching aids.

*   *   *

Unfortunately, there are those who love a good story and enjoy embroidering everything they hear. It was soon getting round the parish that I'd gone to Alice's house demanding her resignation.

But Alice knew better. I was honest with her about the comments made at the meeting and made it quite clear I had no intention of asking her to resign.

The grace with which she received my news, and the honesty with which we were able to talk things over, moved me deeply. I also knew by the end of our chat exactly what I would say at the next church council meeting, which for various reasons had to be put off until October.

Meanwhile, Alice and Mary kept Sunday School going each week until August. On the second Sunday in September they met again and the children learnt a lovely hymn which they sang at Harvest. The church was packed, and this paved the way for the fortnightly family service.

*   *   *

I asked Alice if she'd mind coming a bit later to the next church council meeting. I think she guessed why.

Having reminded them that it was they, not I, who'd been pressing for Alice to resign, I pointed out that I had given no such undertaking at that meeting and had no intention of doing so. I also told them I considered it pretty feeble that, having known about Alice's problems, not one of them had offered to help her.

Before anyone could interrupt I said that although everyone kept saying Sunday School was putting people off church for life, I'd calculated that of the seventy adults at the Harvest Service no less than forty were once in Alice's class. What was more, three-quarters of the Church Council had been taught by her.

After a lot of embarrassed shuffling Emma Hammerford and Mrs Small admitted they'd been a bit hasty, and when Alice walked

45

into the hall I was relieved to see everyone giving her a friendly welcome.

For fifty-seven years she'd taught and now, thanks to some help from outside the parish, the Sunday School was taking on a new lease of life.

As far as I was concerned Alice was fifty-seven, not out.

Chapter 8

It's Taken You Long Enough

"Diddn' you know 'e's been in 'ospital with a stroke for four weeks? The family's been at 'is bedside day and night for the last seven days."

Peter Eastridge was holding forth in the middle of the village street, thoroughly enjoying the fact I knew nothing of the illness of James Stevens. Now he had a chance to get his own back on me. I prepared myself for a lecture on my shortcomings, but Peter's mind went off in another direction and a smile of triumph spread across his face. "'Tis that Will Swift's fault. Fine churchwarden 'e is! Lives next door to poor old James and never said aught 'bout'n."

While it was true one or two of their fields were adjacent, James' and Will's houses were in fact miles apart and approached from different directions.

Within minutes of getting home, Mr Oswald, the undertaker, phoned to say Mr Stevens was dead. He warned me that the family was very upset because I had not been near the hospital.

Five minutes later Colonel Waters was on the line. "You must have known about James. Everyone in the parish knew how ill he was. People said how funny it was you didn't pray for him on Sunday. Mr Turner would never have . . ."

Months had gone by without anyone reminding me of my predecessor. It was my second March in Ashenridge and during the previous twelve months nearly every home in the parish had received a visit from me. Stories of my attempts to help people like Kitty may

47

have enhanced my reputation, and I was aware that my more relaxed style in leading church worship was appreciated by most. But it looked like my honeymoon period was over.

"But he does seem very young to have suffered such a serious a stroke," I protested. "He didn't look more than fifty when I saw him in his farmyard a few months ago."

"No, rector, he was eighty-seven. The man you saw at the farm was probably Harry, his nephew."

*   *   *

I remembered clearly my first visit to Withy Farm, the home of James Stevens. I was not impressed by the man with the rat-like face I encountered in the yard. I assumed he was the owner. At the time he was in the process of pulling down an ancient cob barn. On seeing me approach, he deliberately called the men away from their tea break to start work again. During the brief interview that followed he sat on a noisy tractor, shouting to the lads and occasionally throwing remarks in my direction. He made it clear he had no time for the church, and being made to feel thoroughly unwelcome I left.

*   *   *

I was just leaving the church when, to my dismay, I spotted the broad figure of Ned Hooper, the dahlia grower, leaning over the church gate smoking his morning pipe. Ned was not noted for brief conversations. He always seemed to have limitless hours to while away and assumed his listeners were equally glad to fill their time.

With his walrus moustache and big bushy eyebrows he beamed at me. "'Tis a fine day, rector," he began. "You'm lucky, someone with lots of time just like me. Why, I was just thinkin' what 'twas like when Mr Turner was 'ere."

I knew I was in for it. My training had taught me that a clergyman must always appear to have time to listen no matter how busy he may actually be. Now that notion was about to be put to the test. For what seemed like half a day I submitted to hearing about the great deeds of my predecessor. How people came from miles around to attend his popular services; how his choir was noted for its wonderful singing. He was a great resolver of differences in the community and ran wonderful Sunday School outings. Thanks to him every village function flourished.

I was getting desperate, but short of being rude there was no way of interrupting. The final straw came when he pointed to the churchyard. "Why, Mr Turner would spend hours out there talking to people. He could tell you the life story of everyone 'e'd buried there."

"You'll enjoy this one," he continued, waving his pipe at me and about to launch into another of his long stories. Desperate, I broke in. "Ned, forgive me, but you'll have to leave that one for another day. I'm afraid I'm in a hurry to call on a bereaved family. What's more I'm in trouble because nobody told me one of them had been on the point of death for four weeks."

"'Ere, steady on," Ned replied. "You'm in no hurry. You'm not like me. All my life I've worked six days a week, proper 'ard work. You just works the one, and you thinks you'm working 'ard."

"Come off it, Ned," I retorted. "Do you think that funerals and caring for the bereaved are just a pastime? Do you think I simply amuse myself conducting weddings and Confirmation classes?"

Ned was still not taking things in, so I continued half jokingly, "Perhaps you think I relax by running all kinds of parish organisations, dealing with pressing problems or distressed people? Do you suppose I just wander into the church to take a service with no thought beforehand? And remember, it's not just one parish. What's more, just at this moment the Stevens family are expecting me now that James has passed away."

"James Stevens!" cried a shocked Ned, nearly swallowing his pipe. "James Stevens! Why didn' you say so afore? 'Ere you shouldn't be making me stand 'ere talking when there's folk to see." Then, drawing in his breath he added, "Fancy that, cousin James gone."

*   *   *

Sullen Harry was waiting for me. He emerged from the Dutch barn which stood on the site of the recently-destroyed cob building.

"It's taken you long enough to show an interest in poor old uncle," was the best he could offer. "But now you're here, I suppose you'd better come in."

Inside I found a tearful Mrs Stevens being comforted by several familiar faces from the village. I recognised her brother because he farmed in the parish. Her two married sisters both lived in cottages in Ashenridge. Eight pairs of eyes were looking disapprovingly at me.

"Well at least you're here now," was how Mrs Stevens responded to my profuse apologies for not knowing about her husband's illness. On checking the date when James fell ill I realised I'd been deeply involved in the problems of Kitty and her family at the time. In a community like this, if you're not talking to the right person at the right time you miss the news and everyone assumes you know what's been going on.

I wondered why the nurses at Leighford Hospital hadn't told me James was a patient there. Normally they would let me know if they were tending anyone from my parishes. Later I discovered that out-lying Withy Farm was on their records as Westaleigh parish, hence nothing was said. Not being a mind reader, there was no earthly way of knowing about James's illness. This, however, was not the time for explanations, so I meekly submitted to the family's disapproval.

At a funeral I always like to say something about the deceased. Unfortunately my proddings produced nothing of any value. Their reaction was that if I wasn't interested in James while he was alive, why should I be interested now? How different it would have been had Mr Turner still been around. As for that wonderful hospital chaplain, why he'd been at James's bedside every day.

"Look, why don't you ask Mr Turner to come back and take the funeral? I'm sure he would be glad to come out of retirement for this occasion as he knows you so well. Or you could ask the hospital chaplain."

My suggestion was followed by an embarrassed silence, then after a long pause Mrs Stevens said, "No, we think you ought to take the funeral. After all, you're the rector."

*   *   *

Next day the undertaker, Mr Oswald, called on me. He was in a bit of a stew. He told me the whole family was hurt by what I'd said. I was accused of asking a lot of nosy questions about their affairs. And they reckoned I didn't want to conduct the funeral because I'd suggested someone else.

Mr Oswald's words astonished me.

I asked him where all this had come from. I should have guessed, it was Harry. Mr Oswald knew very little about the family, they tended to keep themselves to themselves, but when someone took on the role of family spokesman, as Harry had, he felt he must take his words seriously.

In an attempt to put things right I said, "I know you're going to Withy Farm this afternoon. Would you do me a favour and talk to Mrs Stevens for me? Tell her I'm more than willing to conduct the funeral."

*   *   *

My next move was to see Peter Eastridge. I knew he was a close family friend and I hoped he'd help sort things out. Peter looked awkward as I poured out my tale. He said very little but promised to do what he could. I sensed his inward glow of satisfaction because I'd gone to him for help.

I returned home to a frantic Mary. The phone had been going non-stop about the funeral. Having had the record put straight by the undertaker *and* Peter Eastridge, Mrs Stevens was very sorry about any misunderstanding. She definitely wanted me to take the funeral.

Peter called next. In confidence he explained there had been a major row in the family. Harry had taken too much upon himself and had been put firmly in his place. An illegitimate nephew, for whom the Stevens had made a home, he'd taken over much of the running of the farm as James and his wife grew older, but there was never any promise that he would inherit it from the childless couple. For that reason he was resentful when anyone else took an interest in the business.

The church was full, and after the funeral I was told that people were taken aback because I actually said a few kind words about James Stevens, something Mr Turner would never have done. I think they approved.

*   *   *

That autumn the church council invited Mr Turner to preach at Harvest. He was so slight a puff of wind would have blown him over. No wonder he'd neglected the rectory garden. At Harvest Supper he told me that of late he'd only visited people who actually lived in the village and then only when asked. He didn't remember the Stevens family at all, or indeed some of the other families who claimed to be his fans. He was surprised when I told him how popular he was.

Later I discovered that the Leighford Hospital Chaplain was actually on holiday for the last two weeks of James Stevens' life. So much for stories about his daily bedside visits!

Chapter 9

You Can't Take It With You

At first I didn't notice it . . . the battered blue van parked outside Bert Hopkins' cottage in the middle of the village. Little did I know what trouble it was going to cause.

To anyone visiting the West Country, Ashenridge consists of a mix of ancient cob and thatched cottages mingled with slightly newer houses built of stone and slate. There had been houses here ever since people first walked the ancient ridge road along which the village was built. Most of the older properties were well preserved. Others still suffered from neglect, thanks to the depression and the war years, and Bert's was one of them.

I was so preoccupied on this particular day that I barely noticed Len's nod as he walked by, or the menacing look from Peter Eastridge as he drove past. The truth was I felt very depressed.

Twenty months ago Ashenridge had offered me a great challenge. Here were people with real needs. The sick; the bereaved; the confused; the anxious, and those seeking some real purpose in their lives.

Amongst other things I was becoming an expert at countersigning application forms, but that wasn't really why I was here. I still had a strong desire to meet people's real needs, no matter what their view of God or the church.

This morning I felt disillusioned. Some residents had an insatiable appetite for talking about the weather. Another villager whose wife lay dead upstairs was only interested in his tomato crop. Yet another old chap, knowing he was at death's door, was more concerned about how much of his money would be needed for the funeral than where he would spend eternity.

As I continued down the street I missed the significance of that van. My mind was full of the latest threat to me – Westaleigh. I knew its ageing vicar was about to retire, and the bishop wanted to add it to my other two parishes.

More than one person had commented, "If you think you've got problems here, you should try working in Westaleigh." I was not anxious to try. I was failing badly enough where I was.

"I'm not asking you to handle Westaleigh on your own," the bishop had said. "I'm keen to send a young man straight from college to gain experience with you. Too many clergy only know about towns and are a disaster in the countryside. They just don't understand the people. With your rural background I'm confident you'd be the ideal person to train him."

This should have encouraged me. Instead the thought of taking on a curate and enthusing him chilled me. Just now I was the one who needed encouraging. What was more, I knew that having sent me a curate the bishop would not be content with simply adding one more parish to my quota. Others would certainly follow.

The noise of a tractor brought me back to reality. It's driver was trying to negotiate a large trailer round the blue van outside Bert Hopkins' cottage. It was then I remembered seeing it there the previous week. Bert was not the sort of person to keep calling in a builder. He was much happier just sitting in his armchair, smoking a pipe and letting the fire in the hearth warm his slippered feet.

Years ago Bert had been gamekeeper on the Ashenridge estate and the cottage had been left to him in the squire's will. The squire was long gone. So was Ashenridge Hall, an early nineteenth-century house which barely lasted a hundred years before having to be demolished after a terrible fire. At Bert's cottage alone something of the mansion survived in the shape of furniture rescued from the flames. In fact, so much had been jammed into it that Bert's big downstairs room seemed quite small. A large kitchen table stood in the middle of the room. Its main function was to hold the odd plant, Bert's cap and goodness knows how many secondhand copies of *Horse and Hound*. The rest of the room was full of settees and armchairs, most of which were never used. The walls were lined with dusty chests and cupboards. On the smoke-stained walls were displays of shotguns, hunting prints and a hanging clock with swinging pendulum. This clock had always been in Bert's family and was one of his prized possessions.

"I should think they'll do well there," said Annie Cook, pointing at the van with her crooked finger. "They've been all round the village buying things. Been giving several shillings for old lamps . . . the ones we used before the electric light came here. He even paid £5 for Ned's old grandfather clock. It was all worn out, hadn't gone for forty years. Helpful he was, too. Didn't fancy any of the furniture Flossie Bluett tried to sell him. He didn't want to disappoint her, so he cleared out an old shed so she could put her chickens there. He gave her thirty shillings for the lot. Old chimney crooks, fire dogs and the like. I don't know, fancy wanting to buy things like that."

As we stood talking I saw a man come out of Bert's house and drive away. I felt it wise to investigate. He was unlikely to be buying fire irons. Bert always had a big 'stick' burning in his hearth, surrounded by all kinds of appliances hanging down from an iron framework in the chimney. His was one of the few really large open fires still to be found in the village. He used to boast that he did all his cooking on this fire, although everyone knew that Millie, a wonderful next-door neighbour, always brought him in a cooked Sunday lunch and other meals during the week.

Sitting in an armchair on the opposite side of the fire from Bert, my eyes gradually adjusted. Nothing seemed to be missing. The fire irons were still in place, the clock ticking on the wall. The fusty room smelt of smoke, unwashed clothes and Bert's pipe, which lived perpetually between his teeth.

Soon the story came out. "Fust time 'e comes, 'e offers me £5 for the clock. Us told 'un what 'e could do with 'is £5. Whatever 'tus worth, us'll not part with 'un. Back 'e comes today and offers me £10. My durr soul! Us told 'un thut were no good. Then 'e starts nosin' round. Us says 'e can 'ave thut old chair in the corner thut was squire's. But 'e weren't interested in 'un. Seemed a nice sort of chap, though. 'E told me 'bout all they places 'e goes to, and 'ow 'ard times be, though us don't think they'm as bad as 'e makes out. All the while 'e was lookin' round the room. Then 'e made as if to go off. Just as 'e comes to the door, 'e says '£10 for the rosewood cabinet be'ind the sofa'. Leastways that's what us thought 'e sayed."

Behind the sofa, wedged between chests and chairs, Bert pointed to a delicately made cabinet with a glass front and black velvet-lined shelves. There appeared to be nothing in it. As far as I could see the sides and legs were made of attractive turned rosewood. The top was covered with a faded cloth on which stood various shooting cups won by Bert in the 1920s.

"Us don't know what to do 'bout 'n," said Bert. "'E's back next Wednesday for to see whut us'll say. My durr soul, never know'd us 'ad anything valuable 'yurr. Most of this 'yurr stuff comes out of squire's kitchen. Us is sure 'e never kept 'is valuables there."

I was not so sure. The story sounded familiar. A dealer looks all round a house, dismisses everything, then makes a quick offer for something apparently worthless just so the person is not disappointed. I told Bert to wait until I came back.

That evening I rang a friend who knew quite a lot about antiques. He was horrified when I told him about the price given for fire irons and oil lamps. When I described the rosewood cabinet, he assured me it could be worth quite a lot, depending on its condition. It looked sound enough to me. He told me it might be worth as much as £100, but rather than raise Bert's expectations too much, he suggested I tell him it was worth at least £25 and he must have nothing to do with the dealer.

Next day I took the news to Bert who promised he would send the dealer away. He was so grateful for my help he presented me with a picture of a stag at bay. The poor animal looked pitiful. The frame was mouldy and the print fly spotted. I didn't fancy having it at the rectory and I knew Mary would hate it. However, Bert insisted and made it impossible for me to refuse his gift.

As I carried the picture home it began to slip from under my arm. I tried to steady it with my other hand and then discovered the backing was completely rotten. My fingers went right through it. With great care I withdrew them but to my horror discovered a part of the picture was stuck to my thumb.

*   *   *

The first thing I knew about my upsetting Bert was when a very smug Peter Eastridge appeared on my doorstep announcing that Bert would not be giving a prize to the Christmas draw.

Peter was a bit cautious about what he said to my face – after all he still hoped to become a churchwarden one day. By stirring things up he hoped to make my stay in the parish a short one. He'd actually been very helpful over the Stevens family, but now he was back to his old self. I think part of his problem was controlling his jealousy. After all, we were both farmer's sons. While he was struggling on an antiquated farm, I had an easy job, a splendid house and, as he wrongly supposed, a high income.

On this occasion jealousy won the day and Peter could hardly hide the look of triumph on his face. "Didn't you know poor old Bert thinks you're trying to swindle him?"

Before I had a chance to say anything he made off down the drive muttering "And I don't blame 'im."

*   *   *

"Us is all right, thankin' you all the same, but us'd rather you didn' call." I could tell from the way Bert was standing I was not meant to cross the threshold.

"Whatever's the matter, Bert?" I asked.

"'Tus no good comin' 'yurr," he said. "Us wants you to know us'll 'ave no more to do with your church."

"But last time we talked you were thankful for the help I gave you."

"'Elp, call that 'elp? My durr soul! Why you'm no better than they

57

dealers. Offerin' me £25 for me precious rosewood cabinet, and you knowed all the time."

"What did I know?"

"Why, 'twas worth four times thut. Us got a proper dealer, one us can trust, and thut's what 'e sayed. If thut's 'ow you runs a church us wants nothin' more to do with un."

I tried to explain about the valuation, but he wasn't listening. He just kept repeating, "Fancy sayin' 'twas only worth £25. My durr soul."

As I walked away I heard him mutter, "'An' Millie says 'twas very wrong you makin' me give you that picture. 'Er reckons thut be worth a lot, too."

Reason would not prevail. Perhaps one day Bert would see things in a better light, but with Peter Eastridge stirring things in the background there seemed little likelihood of that. Had it been possible I would have returned the print, but thanks to the accident there was a gaping hole where the stag's mouth should have been. If Bert were to see his precious print now it would make things even worse.

The only thing I could do was call on Millie. At first she listened politely, uncertain whether or not to believe me. Clearly Peter Eastridge had got his word in first. After a while I found her sympathising with me, especially when I mentioned the incident with the print. What I said rang true. Bert was always pressing things on people they didn't really want. She explained it was Tim, the local fish man, who'd told Bert the real value of his cabinet. In his spare time Tim dabbled in antiques. When I told her why I'd played down the value Millie understood and promised to do her best to pour oil on troubled waters.

Peter Eastridge was determined to make the most of things. He held forth in the Coach and Horses about my iniquities. I knew wild stories were spreading about me cheating old folk. When I heard that Bert was going to bring a lawsuit against me I decided I had no option but to return the picture, no matter what state it was in. It would have been easier to ask Millie to return it, but that would hardly be fair on her.

I prayed hard that Wednesday morning before setting off to see

Bert. Fate seemed against me. Just as I was passing the Coach and Horses who should step out but Peter Eastridge He glared at me and then at the picture. Blowing out his cheeks and with a hint of victory in his eyes he started. "Mornin', rector. I see you'm busy. They say you'm interested in antiques and they reckons you knows a thing or two. I s'pose you've been out visitin' again?"

I felt it was time to confront Peter with the truth and asked him where he got his information from.

"Well you know what they'm sayin' all round the village. They reckons they knows why you'm callin' on people."

"Why do I call on people?"

The veneer of politeness left Peter's face. He turned on me like someone about to pounce on a rat. "I'll tell you why. You show me what you've got in your 'ands." Before I realised what was happening, Peter made a grab for the picture. In his anger he knocked it out of my grasp and it crashed against a large stone on the ground.

"Now look what you've done," I cried.

The remains of Bert's print lay at our feet. The frame was broken, there was glass everywhere, and the stone had made a huge hole in the picture.

Peter bent down in horror. He tried putting the picture together again, then muttered something about it being worthless anyway.

"Yes," I agreed. "Quite worthless. Do you know where it came from? It came from Bert Hopkins. He gave it to me a few weeks ago. I only accepted it to please him. In fact it's been propped in a corner of my study ever since. Now there seems to be some sort of rumour going round the village about my taking a valuable picture from him so I decided the best thing would be to return it."

Peter grabbed an old paper sack from his van and together we began picking up the pieces. As we did so I continued, "Unfortunately Bert seems to have taken a strong dislike to me, otherwise I would have returned it sooner. How fortunate you know Bert so well. In view of what's happened, perhaps you'd be kind enough to return his picture and explain the circumstances." With that I left a very red-faced Peter to sort out the mess.

59

A few months later Bert suffered a stroke and was admitted to Leighford Hospital. Millie, who was now convinced I'd been telling the truth all along, reassured me his attitude had softened and he'd like me to visit him. Furthermore, there was no need to worry because he'd promised her the rosewood cabinet when he was gone.

After his stroke Bert's speech was a bit slurred, but he was getting some of the use back in his left hand. After a few minutes I noticed tears in his eyes and he slowly explained he didn't want to leave this world before putting things right. He realised I was only trying to do the best for him and was sorry for what he'd said, only people were confusing him. It was that Peter Eastridge who'd suggested I was trying to swindle him. At least that's what he thought he was saying.

Leaning towards me he whispered, "When us be gone, us wants for you to 'ave thut cabinet, 'tus yours.'"

"That's very kind of you, Bert, but I thought you wanted Millie to have the cabinet?"

His face began to contort and I feared he was going into a spasm, but he calmed down again. "My durr soul you'm right, 'twas Millie. Or 'twas it Joey . . . or 'twas it Tim?"

I asked Bert if he'd made a will and suggested we ask his solicitor to put something in writing about the cabinet. He reckoned he didn't have much time left and was worried about his possessions. I gently reminded him that he should perhaps be thinking more about the things to come than the things he was leaving behind.

"You'm right," he said. "You can't take it with you."

I needn't have bothered ringing the solicitor. That night Bert had another stroke and died.

*   *   *

The first anyone knew about it was when a smartly dressed solicitor's clerk from Leighford appeared on the scene. He collected the key from a tearful Millie and on behalf of Bert's next of kin, a distant nephew, took charge of the house. He even got someone to change all the locks.

He explained to Millie that he'd been instructed to sell the contents of the house. The proceeds were to go to the nephew. If Millie wanted the rosewood cabinet she would have to bid for it at the local auction. An astonished Joey was told the same. So was Tim. All three had been promised the cabinet!

*　　*　　*

The church was packed for Bert's funeral. At the service I spoke of his love of the old days when he worked at the manor and his pride in having all the furniture the squire left him. He was a man of high principles who hated dishonesty. He really did value the soul God had given him.

To ease tension at a funeral, especially when someone has lived to a ripe old age, I try to say something to make the mourners smile. On this occasion I quoted Bert's favourite phrase 'my durr soul'. I noticed Millie, sitting in the front pew, smiling and crying at the same time.

*　　*　　*

Three days later Millie was invited to Bert's house. The solicitor's clerk said, "It's all right, you can have the rosewood cabinet, that's if you really want it. It's over there."

In one corner of the room lay a heap of glass and worm-eaten wood. Bereft of other furniture to support it, Bert's rosewood cabinet had disintegrated!

Chapter 10

Fresh Hope?

Sitting in the front row of Ashenridge Church on the first Sunday of 1959 was a tall, red-faced man in his early thirties. He was clearly enjoying the service. He sang with enthusiasm and listened carefully to my sermon. He appeared like a ray of sunshine during a low period in my ministry when everything seemed to be going wrong.

*   *   *

As the days had got darker and darker that previous autumn, I'd seemed to be walking through some endless gloomy tunnel. I kept wondering whether I was a total failure. Angry though Peter Eastridge was about not being churchwarden, was he more perceptive about my shortcomings than I realised? Was the cynical Jim Stillman really only uncovering the truth when he wrote the church off 'for what it's worth'? Was I the fool my dark-suited contemporaries hinted at when I opted to bury myself in the countryside?

Events at Christmas had helped me forget my troubles. The mini-pantomime put on by the village school was a great success with Paul taking part as a budding conjurer and Ann as a fairy. Carol singing was great fun and we were given a particularly warm welcome at some of the more remote homes. One farmer was so beside himself with delight he made us wait while he cut huge rounds of beef sandwiches followed by delicious slabs of Christmas cake. The children's lemonade had certainly kept out the cold, having had something unusually warming mixed with it!

The family enjoyed Christmas and on the days that followed Mary and I took Paul and Ann on some good walks. It was also our first Christmas with television, thanks to the generosity of my parents. 'Dixon of Dock Green', Tony Hancock, Ted Ray, Charlie Drake and a host of others could be seen in our home through this modern miracle.

Going to church early in the new year was like coming round after an anaesthetic. I had to face the fact that the congregation, which had grown during my early days, was now dwindling. Even on Christmas morning numbers had been less than the previous year. The choir, which a year ago had seemed to be mushrooming, was now reduced to a faithful few.

Excuses for absence were manifold. They ranged from "I'm sorry, rector, but my father comes to lunch on a Sunday" to "But I have to get ready to go to town on Mondays." Some excuses took more believing than others.

Church seemed to come last on most people's lists of priorities, unless it was a wedding or some other special occasion. How sad I'd felt on Christmas morning to see one member of our church council taking a stroll rather than coming to church. Not only did this affect me, it also discouraged others. How could they grumble about young people not coming to church when they didn't bother themselves? What message were we sending out when Sunday lunch and going to town on a Monday were more important than God?

I could not escape the truth, I was failing. If it continued like this, things would be worse than when I first came to Ashenridge.

*　　*　　*

The young man sitting in church that morning turned out to be Rufus Atkins. He sat in the rectory after the service warming his hands round a cup of coffee and told me he was a local government officer, just starting in a new post at Leighford, and was lodging here in Ashenridge. A recent convert, he was full of zeal with strong views on all kinds of subjects. He deplored nuclear war. He would exchange organs for guitars in church. His views about conservation were ahead of his time and I knew they would put him at odds with the local farmers who were still grubbing up old orchards and tearing down ancient hedges.

On the strength of a commendation he brought from his previous church I gave him a warm welcome. In next to no time he took over the small youth club Mary and I ran. Given the chance he would have taken over the whole church, and I actually found myself trying to cool some of his enthusiasm because none of us could cope with all his ideas at once.

"You're clutching at straws," Mary warned me. "Don't put all your faith in him. Try him and prove him first."

Even our children were wary of him. They may have joined in some of his activities, but they were still cautious.

I was aware of some of Rufus' shortcomings. He had a habit of saying how God had healed him, yet this seemed to be the sum total of his faith. He resisted any suggestions of mine to spend more time in prayer and personal bible reading.

But most youngsters loved Rufus, and the youth club grew until it drew in practically every young person living in and around the parish. January that year was bitterly cold, so one Saturday he gathered together an army of teenagers to collect wood, chop it up and then distribute logs to the homes of pensioners. One weekend they had a litter hunt and burnt all the rubbish on a huge bonfire.

Rufus also organised a football match against a neighbouring youth group and I went along to the playing field to support our team. At half-time Len Cooksley told me how, as a youngster, he'd been a keen footballer. In later years he'd travelled quite a distance by coach so he could support his home team.

"Twas such a funny road, all different. You goes up it, but don' 'e try comin' back down on 'un . . . leastways not unless you wants an accident. Then us comed back t'other way. You musn' try goin' back the same way. Seemed all baxi-forward to me, only 'twas sensible really."

Realising I was getting quite lost he began all over again. "Tis like this. You goes up one way, then you comes back t'other, only 'tisn't the same road. You've got little things like walls to keep you in."

Pointing with his hands one way and then the other, he continued. "You goes this way, and they goes that way, otherwise they'll crash. Only 'tis all on the same road as 'twere, leastways that's how I reckons 'tis."

I was beginning to cotton on. "Len, you're talking about a dual carriageway."

"That's right, a jewel something. Oh, talkin' 'bout that, look what I found in church." With that he placed a medal in my hand.

"It belongs to the gentleman up to Ashenridge 'Ouse. I promised I'd get it back to 'im. 'E wore it for the army sticks."

I couldn't help smiling. Remembrance Sunday, or Armistice Day as it was known to many of the elderly parishioners, was an important day in Ashenridge.

After the match I looked in at Ashenridge House, a 1920s-style villa on the outskirts of Ashenridge and home to Steven and Sylvia Watson. Steven was a prominent surgeon at Whiteminster General Hospital. Although a professed agnostic, he always made a point of attending the Remembrance Service.

He was grateful to have the medal returned and over a drink talked a little about his job. The conversation turned to healing and, remembering Rufus' views, I suddenly had a flash of inspiration. "I've recently started a monthly discussion group. If I was to have one on the subject of healing, would you come?"

He agreed, and when I told Rufus about the proposed discussion he jumped at the chance to talk about his favourite subject.

The group met monthly at the rectory and was the one thing that was going reasonably well. I was beginning to break new ground, drawing in some folk who did not regularly attend church. For the first time people were beginning to feel free to talk openly about their faith. Things did not always work out as I expected. One evening our subject was about the sacraments. This set Len off talking with deep

65

feeling about the 'supreme sacrament'. Soon we all realised he meant 'sacrifice', as in the two world wars, and the rest of the evening was filled with people talking about their wartime experiences. I felt we were achieving something here, and I was hoping the next meeting would attract more people. It did.

*   *   *

A fortnight later the rectory was bursting at the seams. More than thirty people had turned up. I started by talking about passages in the Bible which spoke of Jesus' ministry to the sick. Rufus then rushed in with his own experience. He put it in such a way as to imply Christians only used doctors when their faith was weak. This brought a quick retort from Steven who stressed that we must not take all Bible healing stories literally. From then on Rufus and Steven monopolised the meeting and no matter how hard I tried I could not persuade the others to join in.

Rufus insisted that if God promised to heal then He was bound to keep His word, otherwise He was virtually a fraud. He told stories of people recently healed from cancer, and cripples throwing away their crutches. He waxed lyrical about people with their sight restored and others released from mental depression. It was inspiring stuff. As he spoke of God's work I remembered seeing remarkable things happen in military hospitals after prayer. Indeed, such experiences had contributed to my calling to the ministry.

Then Steven launched forth. Many of the miracles in the Bible had perfectly simple scientific explanations. Other healings could be explained psychologically. Quite clearly God did not put people right every time they asked. Steven described some terrible deaths. If there was a God at all, then He was remote and unfeeling. Rufus was simply being naive.

I could appreciate Steven's point. God did not always answer our prayers, at least not as we expected. At college we were trained to have a realistic and scientific approach towards life. We must not be Bible literalists. In this case, there was truth on both sides.

Rufus retorted by quoting Bible texts. 'Ask and you shall receive.' To try and balance the argument I commented that Jesus did not automatically cure everybody. I reminded them of the crowd of sick people whom Jesus found waiting at the Pool of Bethesda. Jesus only took one person and made him better – why?

Rufus paused, momentarily deflated.

This gave Steven the upper hand. "Your's is a cruel God," he said, glaring at Rufus. "How can He heal some people and ignore the suffering of others? You just haven't begun to understand."

Rufus could bear it no longer. He shouted at Steven, rebuking him for insulting God. He accused him of being an agnostic because he refused to believe anything he could not grasp with his tiny mind. Then he turned on me. "I thought you would have supported me. You're supposed to be a man of God. How can you allow him to say this sort of thing? No wonder your church is so empty. No wonder young people won't come near. If that's the best you can do, I'm going to a proper church where people really believe."

With that Rufus walked out.

*   *   *

Two things happened the next morning. First, I received a letter from the bishop offering me Westaleigh in addition to my two other parishes. The second took place before I had a chance to take in the first. The telephone rang. On the other end of the line was an angry Peter Eastridge. He wanted to know if I was aware that Rufus Atkins had been killed in a road accident early that morning, "You know, the man you upset so much at your meeting last night." I was profoundly shaken.

As the morning wore on it emerged that an eyewitness saw his car skid off the road and go straight into a tree. Rufus was driving like a madman. Whatever insinuations Peter Eastridge might or might not be making round the village, I was convinced it was entirely my fault. Perhaps I should have gone round after the meeting to talk to Rufus. I was haunted by that terrible 'if only I had done so and so' feeling, which affects so many people in times of tragedy.

With some relief I heard that the funeral would take place at Rufus' home in Essex. I telephoned his distraught parents. In a later conversation they said he always drove too fast. They'd kept on warning him that one day he would come to grief. Sadly, Rufus' zeal was matched by his impatience.

Like a nightmare that Sunday came and went. In the services I said very little. We prayed for Rufus and his family and on the pretext of it being cold I sent the congregation home from both churches without an address. My stalwarts were very understanding, especially those who'd been at the meeting.

Len Cooksley did his best to comfort me.

"Don'ee worry, sir. Don'ee take no notice of what Peter Eastridge claims people is sayin'. You know what 'e's like. When 'e says 'they'm sayin', 'e means what 'e's sayin', and when 'e says 'e', 'e usually means 'they'."

I was deeply touched. Despite his gift for making the simple sound so complicated his funny expressions often made me laugh, but he was no fool and a real friend in times of trouble.

*　　*　　*

Steven Watson rang early on the Monday morning. He'd been away over the week-end and was devastated to hear of Rufus' accident. He was at the rectory in a matter of minutes. He could see I blamed myself for what had happened.

"Jack, I understand how you feel. I want to tell you about a young surgeon I knew. He'd been in practice for about two years when he was faced with a delicate operation. In the course of it he made a small mistake and the patient died. Like you, he was devastated, blamed himself. He was going to tender his resignation, but was persuaded by his friends to sleep on it. That night he had a dream. In it he saw himself standing at the gates of heaven. He was telling St Peter he was not worthy to enter because he'd killed a patient. St Peter led him into a room full of people. 'Look at these people,' St Peter said. 'Every one of them has at some stage been healed by you. Do you really think you are no good?' That young surgeon did not give up. He devoted his whole life to his work and was all the more dedicated as a result of his mistake. Through his skills thousands of sufferers were healed. Jack, you must believe that in your own way you are doing the same here. You may not see me in church that often, but I do hear about the people you've helped.

What's more, he continued, you may feel a complete failure over Rufus, but from what I've heard you were a steadying influence on a very headstrong man. I'm afraid I was a bit of a Devil's advocate the other night, but Rufus had to learn that people are entitled to their views. In fact I have witnessed miraculous cures and I do believe they can actually happen. This was the card I held up my sleeve, but Rufus never gave me the chance to use it."

It took the words of an agnostic to bring me to my senses. I learnt in later days to be grateful to God for allowing me to reach such a low point in my ministry. I was able to use the experience again and again to help others when they hit rock bottom in their lives.

*   *   *

A week after the disastrous meeting I wrote to the bishop accepting the parish of Westaleigh.

Chapter 11

Taking A Day Off

Steven Watson's words were ringing in my ears. "If you don't have some time off you'll end up useless to yourself and everyone else."

My father always boasted he'd never had a holiday in his life except three days for a honeymoon. "Farmers, true countrymen, don't take days off," he used to say.

"Oh, don't they?" Mary challenged me. "I seem to remember seeing your father and brother sitting in the kitchen in the afternoon listening to the Test Match. Then there were all those days at the market. Don't tell me they spent all their time on business. And what about following the hunt? I know you didn't, but how many times did the others go off all day, leaving you to run the farm?"

"Mum, Dad, can I have a pony and go riding?" piped in a hopeful Ann, half hearing our conversation.

"We could never afford it," I retorted hastily.

"That's what you always say, Dad. We can never afford anything. All my friends have parents who take them out to do all kinds of exciting things. But not you, you're always too busy. Church on Sunday and some awful parish do on Saturdays. It isn't fair. And sometimes in the evenings you send me and Paul to our room because you have some horrible meeting downstairs. I wish you were more like a normal father who has fun with his family. You're horrible."

I couldn't get away from it. The family and Steven Watson were right. I lived for my work morning, noon and night. Mary was not the only one saying I was married to the parish.

A few mornings later I went for a walk, determined to put my resolution into practice. I followed a track near home which led over fields towards a cover which promised shortly to be carpeted with bluebells. I envied the cattle as they calmly munched in the spring sunshine, untroubled by the world. Rays of light struck clumps of primrose, dog's mercury and celandines in the banks. If only my ministry was as bright and fresh as them. Deep in thought, I took a different path back towards the village.

"I thought you'd be in church at this time of day. Having a day off?"

Like a startled rabbit, I found myself staring through a gap in the hedge at Colonel Waters. The path I was on ran alongside part of his garden.

I don't know if he expected a reply, but I found myself pouring out my pent-up feelings.

"By Jove, you're right," he said. "Only a fool gets into a rut. You see, rector, you've got to be yourself, not what other people expect you to be. Now look here, there's a Ways and Means meeting tonight, but there's nothing of great importance to talk about. Why not ring Will Swift and tell him it's off? Then go and have a day out with your family."

*   *   *

Back at the rectory I shooed an astonished family into the car. We'd only driven a few yards when Annie Cook's pointed finger stopped our progress. Her reproachful eye gazed at our walking clothes and picnic hamper. She wanted to tell me about one of her neighbours who'd gone down with 'flu.

"I know you like to be told who's ill so you can visit them. Er . . . but I don't want to interfere with your holidays," she added disapprovingly.

Paul begged me to stop by a stream on our journey. He was really interested in nature. The previous year he'd kept a secret collection of frogs in his bedroom until one escaped and landed in Ann's toy cupboard. Having reassured everyone that this year he would keep his pets out of doors, he was hoping to find frogspawn.

On the exposed ridge where Ashenridge lay the weather was bright and blowy, but down here in the sheltered valley it was like a summer's day. Off came duffle coats and out came camping stools for a coffee break. Paul's quest for frogspawn was a failure, so I showed him how to spot fish in the water. Then I taught both children the art of skimming stones.

"Gosh, Dad," Paul exclaimed. "We never thought you knew about things like that. You're always too busy."

I assured them that in future I would be less busy, especially during school holidays. As I did so, I became aware of a van pulling up.

"Mornin' Mr Longfield," said a familiar voice. "See you'm on your 'olidays."

To my astonishment it was Peter Eastridge. He must have been fifteen miles from home, yet here he was as large as life.

"Funny thing," he continued. "Us was coming to see you when us'd finished work."

"How come you're here?" I asked.

Peter took pride in pointing to some nearby land he owned, and ended very pointedly by saying it was about four times the distance between Ashenridge and Combe Peter, "And us comes every day to see our flock."

"Any roads, 'twas to warn you about that Swift. 'E's makin' real trouble with poor old Mrs Mansell next door." With that he got back in his van, adding with a look of triumph, "But us don't want to spoil the 'oliday, us'll look in another day."

*   *   *

It was bright and sunny the following morning so I decided to put another part of my resolution into practice. I began clearing an enormous thicket of brambles in the vegetable garden where I was planning to grow soft fruit.

My activities did not escape the notice of Annie Cook. She appeared in the garden, her pointed nose and chin accentuated by a straw hat which was pinched to a point in front. In her hand she held a sharp steel trowel, and as she waved it about in a quite dangerous fashion she summoned me back to my duties by adding a few more names to my 'sick list'. "Oh, but as you're still on your holidays, I won't disturb you," she concluded.

*　　*　　*

I made my way to Watern Farm, wondering if I would find Peter Eastridge at home. I was in luck. Instead of being in some remote corner of his empire, he was sitting in the kitchen, his eyes glued to his latest toy, a 12-inch television set.

"'Tis like this," he explained, taking up the point from our last meeting. "That Swift's no good. You knows Betty Mansell, 'er as lives in the cottage 'alf way down 'is lane. Comed there after 'er 'usband died. Moved out of the old farm'ouse. Didn't want to live in the village, so Swift's people let 'er 'ave this 'ouse.

"Well, when Swift was 'ome, 'e was always lookin' in at 'er 'ouse pretendin' to 'elp and do things for 'er. Only what 'e really wanted was 'er things. 'Er's got no children, and nobody to leave things to. Then 'e started bangin' at night. Fair frightened the livin' daylight out of 'er. Now 'e's got a chicken 'ouse just by 'er, and 'tis fair stinkin' the place out. Fine churchman 'e is. 'E goes nowhere near 'er nowadays, and 'er don't know what to expect next. You'd best see what you can do, if you've finished your 'olidays," he added pointedly.

Knowing how much Peter resented Will as churchwarden, I knew I must tread carefully. I went to see Mrs Mansell hoping the true story would unfold without too much prompting. I knew very little about her. On my first visit she'd simply greeted me on the doorstep. She was a nervous person and found conversation difficult.

Once again she greeted me on the doorstep. Her pale face was framed by a green woollen hat dragged down over straggly grey hair. She looked at me as if to say 'I'm busy'. Noticing a brilliant orange azalea growing near the door, I said, "Why, that's the finest azalea I've seen in years."

Taken off guard she stepped outside to look at it. I complimented her work on the garden, and asked how long she'd been growing the various shrubs. She was quite impressed by my interest, saying several times, "Do you really think I've done a good job?"

Then she decided that, washing day or not, it was time for a cup of tea, and asked if I'd like to join her?

"I suppose you see something of Mr Swift?" I asked, casually.

"Well, not lately," she replied in her slight West Country drawl. "As a matter of fact I asked him not to come so much. Not that I'm complaining about all the jobs he did for me, only it was the things that went missing . . . cutlery, tools, teapots. Mark you, I don't know that he stole them, but each time he left something else seemed to go. When I said this to him, I know he was hurt. He didn't say anything, but he hasn't been inside my house since. Then he started putting chickens in that old shed out there. He was up all hours banging around. Now it's done, the stink is terrible. I don't like to say it, but I think he's got it in for me. Do you think I did the right thing?"

"Were you able to talk it over with anyone?" I asked, giving myself time to think matters through.

"Well, no. Since my husband died, I've always been on my own. I didn't want to live in the village, and really I don't know many people. I was brought up on the moor. I've no car, so it's really only the tradesmen I see. The oil man comes here this afternoon, and the shop brings my order on Fridays. Then there's the fish man and the baker. But I never say much to them 'cause you never know how far things travel."

While she spoke I noticed her trembling hand absentmindedly putting her empty cup amongst an assortment of things on the cluttered sideboard.

"What did the teapot look like?" I asked, eyeing one that was half-hidden under a collapsed pile of old letters and bills. Sure enough, it was the missing teapot. I could tell at a glance it wasn't difficult for things to disappear in this house.

Leaving behind a cheered if somewhat mystified Betty Mansell, I made my way down the track to Will Swift. A few weeks ago he'd invited me to collect some seed potatoes from him and this gave me a good reason to call.

"The trouble is this," he said, when the subject got round to his neighbour. "She's on her own far too much. She's nobody to talk to and keeps imagining things. She thinks I steal her possessions. She won't talk to me now, not even when I tried to explain I'm only using the shed as an experiment. If it works I'm going to build a proper poultry house at the other end of the farm where it won't affect her at all. She's not looking after herself properly. She's always washing but doesn't eat, and gets up at all kinds of odd hours. I see the light on in the middle of the night sometimes. I'm so afraid she'll upset one of her oil lamps and there'll be a disaster. It's such a pity she'll have nothing to do with me."

*   *   *

As I returned home a plan was forming in my mind, if only I could get the family to agree. Passing through the village I was brought back to reality.

"Oh, I see," said Annie Cook, having again flagged me down with her pointed finger. She was glaring at the seed potatoes on the back seat of the car. "Only when you're working again, I wonder if you could call."

*   *   *

"I've got an idea," I announced to the family at tea-time. "This Saturday, why don't we go out again? It's the last chance before term begins. Let's go up on the moor and see if we can find a herd of deer, then we can drive to the coast. We can make it a wonderful day for someone else as well."

I waited with a brave face for the salvo of objections.

"For Uncle Tiddly?" asked Paul.

"No, for a dear old lady who's lonely and never goes anywhere. She knows the moor inside out."

I chose my words carefully, hoping the moor would appeal to Paul, and that the sweeter side of Ann might like to help a lonely old lady. As it was Paul was convinced old ladies knew nothing about nature, and the thought of some unwanted guest brought out the sour side in Ann.

I stuck to my guns, and that Saturday a pleased if slightly confused Betty Mansell sat in the front seat of our car ready to guide me to the best places for deer spotting. Behind sat a squashed-up family, seething with resentment.

"No, you don't want to go that way for deer at this time of the year, try the hidden combe down there," Betty said.

We did so. Crouching down we crept between gorse bushes until we were only a few yards from a herd of about thirty deer. The stags displayed superb antlers. It was a truly breathtaking experience. As we were downwind the animals seemed unaware of our presence. Betty whispered how to tell the age of the stags by their antlers.

Next we were shown a badger set; buzzards soaring above our heads; animal tracks; hares and other creatures. She also pointed out owl droppings and deer tracks. Our guide might not be sure where she kept things at home, but out here she was a different woman. She missed nothing and kept the family spellbound.

While we were having our picnic, Betty asked, "If you're aiming for the coast, would you mind going through Hollowford. It's only a little way extra, and it's where I was married. I haven't been back in years."

I sensed an icy chill of disapproval from behind and glimpsed Paul's face in the mirror which said it all: 'Church, on the day we're going to the sea. Horrible church again'!

A battered wooden sign with 'church' painted on it pointed past Hollowford Barton to a little green track. This brought us to rusty gates leading into the churchyard. By the gate was a stream full of frogspawn. Paul was in his element.

A tearful Betty Mansell relived her wedding day some forty years before as she gazed at the shabby interior of the church. It was not mustiness she could smell but lilies-of-the-valley from her bridal bouquet. Affectionately she touched the pews, the books, the altar hangings.

"If only I lived nearer I could take these things home and wash them," she said, stroking the grubby linen cloths on the altar. "I love washing. I wish I could clean this place up and make it look like it did on our wedding day.

I came here that day imagining I would have a family to care for and love. I came full of hope, and now I'm left with nothing. I'm so tired of just looking after myself. When we were together on the farm, I spent all my time working for my husband. I never noticed how few friends I had. Then Charles died and it was too late. Who would want to know me now? It was really my fault about Will Swift, and he's the only neighbour I've got. I've been so wrong."

We were a little late getting to the coast, but there was still time for a paddle and a game we called 'Tide Fight' before we left for home. The tide was coming in fast as we all made sandcastles and stuck flags on top. We struggled to prevent the incoming tide from destroying them and it was up to Betty Mansell to judge which was the last flag to fall and declare the winner.

*   *   *

We went home sandy and happy. Betty Mansell had regained something of her lost years, the children had enjoyed themselves more than they'd ever expected. It didn't take much prompting from me for Betty to offer to launder the church linen, and with a little more persuasion she agreed to Will Swift taking her backwards and forwards to the church.

Chapter 12

A Difference Of Opinion

"I can't go back! I can't go back!" sobbed Mabel Waterhead, recovering over a cup of tea in our kitchen. "He'll kill me!"

Cautiously I placed a hand on her shoulder. Her long, curly hair half covered an attractive baby-like face. She warmed to my touch. When she'd got over the worst of her weeping, I said, "Now tell me all about it."

All her husband seemed to want was sex and food. Poor Mabel had neither the inclination for the one nor money for the other.

Her hand closed over mine. She began to hug me. I looked round desperately for Mary, then remembered she was at a Women's Institute meeting. Pulling myself away, I said firmly, "Now Mabel this will never do. If Bill thought you'd been hugging me he really would kill you. If you're in so much danger, why not go home to your Mum and Dad at Westaleigh? I'm sure they'd look after you."

Mabel's tear-stained face gazed up at me as she tried to take in my words. Then she began crying again. "He'll kill me," she wailed.

Keeping my distance I tried turning the conversation. "And what about the children? What's happening to them? Where are they? Can Bill look after them?"

Like someone emerging from a dream, she said, "They haven't gone to bed yet. Bill won't know what to do with them. I shall have to go back. Won't you come with me Mr Longfield?"

"Now Mabel, if Bill saw me taking you back to your house, what do you think he'd say? You go back and put the children to bed and try to calm him down. If things still aren't right, come back tomorrow and tell Mary and me all about it."

Much to my relief Mabel disappeared. There were plenty of tales going round the village about her, and I did not relish the thought of people seeing her leave the rectory at dusk when they knew Mary was out. I may have seemed a little hard, but the Waterheads always over-dramatized their troubles. They both loved attention. She was also putting me in a position which could easily be misunderstood.

Later, Mary and I strolled through the village. All was quiet at the Waterhead's house, the lights were out, and we concluded Mabel was doing her best to please Bill!

*   *   *

"Dad. It's the bishop on the phone," cried an impish-looking Ann next morning. "You'd better hurry, it sounds urgent."

I was not going to be fooled again. Paul and Ann loved having fun with me over phone calls. Last time I'd found myself saying 'sir' to our local butcher. On another occasion I was rather short with the arch-deacon having been told by the children that a rather tiresome villager wanted me to give him a lift into Leighford.

Having just returned from my morning calls, I took my time getting out of the car. I picked up the telephone and, sure enough, the bishop's familiar voice of authority addressed me.

"I have a possible curate for you who could live at Westaleigh. He's thirty-one, married with two daughters. He's had plenty of experience. Brought up in rural Surrey and now doing a curacy at a small resort on the South Coast. He's good with youngsters and gets on well with people generally. I know his father from Central Finance Board meetings in London. He's on holiday for a few days and thought he could come and see you on Thursday."

*   *   *

Despite objections by the churchwardens, Westaleigh Church had eventually come under my pastoral care. No longer would it be an independent parish with its own vicar. In future, an assistant clergyman working under me would be living there. The bishop's intention was not only to bring parishes together, but for me to train younger men to be the country clergy of the future.

Whatever the bishop had told Westaleigh, the parish did not share his vision of the future. Instead, I was mistakenly accused of empire building, and being paid a lot more for it.

In some ways Peter Richardson sounded just right for Westaleigh, although 'rural Surrey' suggested stockbroker territory and cocktail parties, a world far removed from our small farms and country folk. Good though his enthusiasm was for rural parishes, I was well aware the bishop tended to assume that anywhere within sight of green fields was 'rural'.

Things never go to plan. That Thursday morning I wanted to create a good impression on Peter and his family. For once my desk was tidy. The children's things were neatly put away. I was about to remove several pairs of muddy Wellington boots from the front porch when I became aware of an apparition in the drive. Barefoot, wearing a dirty nightdress with a tear down one side, and carrying a near-empty whisky bottle, the distraught figure of Mabel Waterhead was fast approaching our house.

"Mr Longfield," a tearful voice cried out, arms outstretched in my direction. "Mr Longfield! Please help me. I've come like you said."

The Richardsons were due in ten minutes. My heart sank as Mabel made her way into the kitchen leaving behind an aroma of cheap scent and neat whisky. In between sips of tea, she told Mary that Bill was accusing her of having affairs with half the men in the parish. As she got into her stride, I began to edge towards the door. Unfortunately she noticed what I was doing and yelled, "Aren't I important enough? If I ain't good enough for you, I'm off!"

Before Mary and I could do anything, Mabel shot into the hall and was out of the house. By the time we reached the front door she'd vanished. She could hardly have had enough time to get as far as the gate.

Our search had barely begun when a very smart young clergyman with neatly groomed hair stepped out of a spotless black car which he'd parked in our drive. Peter Richardson wore a charcoal grey suit with a matching clerical grey raincoat. He was followed by his wife, Clare, and two daughters. The whole family looked as though they'd stepped out of the pages of *Vogue*.

Relaxing over a cup of coffee, Peter told me how happy they were in their South Coast church with all its activities. He warmed as he told me how much teaching he was getting over at his choir practices, explaining the subtleties of the music and how this brought out the deep meaning of the words they were singing. Two members of his over-eighteen group were now considering ordination. He enjoyed the well-attended services with all their richness and variety.

By way of contrast, nowhere in our parishes could we ever hope to offer anything on this scale. I asked Peter how he would feel if on a Sunday morning he found himself in a very chilly church ministering to a congregation of about eight people, the singing being led by a choir of three elderly ladies who tended to sing flat.

Peter winced a bit, then his face brightened. "That would be a wonderful challenge Just what I want."

At that moment I spotted a dishevelled figure emerging from the bushes near the drawing-room window. Any hopes that she might pass by unnoticed were destroyed when an empty whisky bottle came crashing through the French window. The shocked Richardsons were treated to the sight of a swearing Mabel Waterhead shaking her fists at us. As she did so, the tear in her nightdress ripped even further exposing a part of her body not normally on view to the general public.

"Yes," I said, " there's plenty of challenge in rural ministry."

*   *   *

81

We invited Peter and his family to join us for lunch. That afternoon I planned to show him Westaleigh Church and village, the vicarage and then the other two parishes already in my care. In the course of our tour I also wanted him to meet some of our church leaders. As we got deep into our morning chat he relaxed and opened up. He loved people. He was keen they should have a real living faith. He believed in the importance of prayer and worship.

While all that might be true, I wondered how he would cope with the very simple style of worship in our churches. I feared he would be impatient with our slower ways, or would go over our heads with the 'good church music' of which he was so fond. I could see him trying to train a very rudimentary country choir to sing hymns they would not enjoy, to a congregation that would never appreciate their efforts.

Several times Peter asked me why I was spending so much time with him. His own vicar was usually too busy to talk to him and just left him to get on with things. This young man wanted to learn, and yet in his ministry nobody seemed to have spent time with him. His only help came from a diocesan tutor who made sure he knew all about the 1549 Prayer Book, Mysticism in St Paul, and the fine points of an ancient Christian heresy called Docetism. Left with little further help, Peter was developing into what is sometimes termed the 'Professional Clergyman'.

I began to take to the true Peter. Perhaps the bishop wanted him to come here to face some of the realities of life, but I wondered if he and Clare could ever fit into this culture? The best thing was to let the day take its course. It was a pity things didn't work out as simply as that.

*   *   *

Our tour began with a visit to Westaleigh Church. Approaching the gate we could see the bald-headed figure of Sir William Radlett, the chuchwarden. To be sure of meeting the candidate he was doing his annual labour of love, linseed oiling the main door and porch timbers.

Sir William lived in the Old Vicarage, a house separated from the church by a high wall.

I introduced him to the Richardsons. Both men were keen golfers and got on like a house on fire. To bring some reality into the conversation I began to steer the talk round to Sir William's likes and dislikes. However, at that moment his housekeeper came running along the path with an urgent message from Mary. Mabel Waterhead had just had another row with her husband. Storming out of the house, she'd left behind two howling children and a husband about to end it all with an overdose. I was not so gullible as to accept all this at face value, but it did require urgent action. Sir William told me not to worry. He would take Peter and Clare on the rest of the tour.

*   *   *

By the time I got back to the Waterheads the social worker had been. Anyone who knew more about the case would have realised that a few kind but firm words with Bill would have done the trick. Instead, he'd been rushed into hospital. Having found a neighbour to look after the children, I spent most of the afternoon in the lanes around Ashenridge looking for Mabel. Eventually she turned up three doors away!

*   *   *

The next time I saw the Richardsons was at high tea. They were thrilled with the house at Westaleigh. It was in a lovely spot with stunning views. Peter and Clare seemed ready to move in tomorrow.

Thanks to the Waterhead crisis I was denied the chance of showing the Richardsons round myself. I was annoyed to discover that Sir William, having taken a liking to Peter, had invited as many Westaleigh Church councillors as he could get hold of to an informal meeting with them.

I was put in a very awkward position, needing to be firm with Sir William, yet not wanting to get off to a bad start in the new parish. I let it go ahead, but intended making things very clear to Sir William afterwards. He had to understand we were looking for a curate who needed training, not a fully-fledged vicar.

As the Richardsons had quite a long drive home and their children were getting tired they left immediately after the meeting. I, too, had a journey to make, to the hospital to see Bill Waterhead, so we parted before I had a chance to tell Peter what was really on my mind. I promised I would write to him shortly.

The Richardsons' car had hardly left the drive when the telephone rang. It was Sir William. Was he right in detecting a note of hesitation in my voice at the end of the meeting? Did I not realise that people were quite unanimous that Peter was the right man for the job?

Firmly but politely I tried to make it clear we were not considering an experienced man to look after one parish, but a young, untrained curate. Although the house happened to be in Westaleigh, his work would take him throughout the parishes.

I tried to explain my reservations to Sir William, but he chose to ignore much of what I said. He accused me of blocking the way of a 'first-class man'.

*   *   *

Next morning I awoke with a heavy heart. I talked things over with Mary and we felt it essential the Richardsons come over again. I liked Peter, but I was still unsure he'd be the right man for the job.

Sir William had been thinking, too. First thing in the morning he'd phoned the people who'd been at the meeting and together they decided to get up a petition to the bishop asking for Peter to be appointed.

News of this first reached the rectory when Sir William rang to tell me what was going on. He loved his church and he was simply doing what he felt was his duty. I listened to what he had to say and thanked him for his courtesy in phoning, but I regretted the fact he was taking action before talking things through with me. I concluded by stressing the bishop would not appoint someone over my head.

As I prayed in church that morning I was comforted by a verse in the Psalms which assured me that the Lord would contend for me, and all I needed to do was have trust. At that moment I felt a great sense of relief and reassurance. I left the church leaving my troubles behind me.

* * *

The first ray of hope came later that morning when I happened to meet Sally Hunt outside Ashenridge Post Office. She'd been polishing the brass in Westaleigh Church when the Richardsons were being shown round and overheard all of Peter's planned changes for the choir. She was furious. Normally a peace-loving woman, once stirred there was no stopping her.

Just to add a little fuel to the fire, I commented that all this was most surprising. Was she not aware that Sir William was keen to appoint Peter, that even as we spoke he was getting up a petition to send to the bishop. Seeing the look on Sally's face I knew all was not lost. The Lord had chosen the right person for the job!

The following Monday morning two letters arrived at the bishop's palace, each bearing a Leighford postmark. The first was headed with Sir William's crest. The second came in one of Sally's purple envelopes. They both contained signed petitions and each had a covering letter. One asked the bishop to appoint Peter and to remove Westaleigh from my control. The other, scented with Devon violets, requested the opposite.

* * *

At the Sunday service I noticed a stranger in church. At first I assumed she was a holidaymaker, then I remembered that baby face. It was Mabel Waterhead. To say she looked as if she'd stepped out of the pages of a fashion magazine would have been to exaggerate, but nevertheless the change was dramatic. After the service she slipped some money into my hand. "For the window, rector. Bill and me, we're all right now."

In the middle of the week it was my turn to receive two interesting letters. The first came from the bishop enclosing the two petitions. The second came from Peter.

Peter had prayed hard and thought matters through. He was now aware that if he came here he would have to adopt a very different way of life. When I'd suggested he keep sheep on the lawn he thought I'd been joking. Now he realised I'd meant it. Also, he couldn't see himself spending most of an afternoon at a muddy farm meeting the family and then being shown their livestock. This was not how he saw pastoral care. Reluctantly he wished to withdraw as a candidate for the curacy.

I wrote back thanking him and saying I only wished we could have spent more time together. I felt sure that one day he would find the right place and do well there.

I showed Peter's letter to a much more reasonable Sir William.

In his own time he began. "I remain convinced we should have our own rector at Westaleigh. But if we must join forces with Ashenridge, then I'm glad we'll be doing it under you."

Before leaving I went into Westaleigh Church, and not just to admire the newly-oiled timbers.

Chapter 13

An American in The Parish

I was feeling particularly cheerful as I drove over to see the Williams family. It was a beautiful summer's evening with the sun about to dip behind the dark ridge of hills to the west. The farm was on the outskirts of Westaleigh and I'd been asked to call in because Angela and Jerry wanted to discuss the forthcoming Confirmation of their fourteen-year-old son, Simon.

Turning into their tree-arched lane, I noticed the track had been concreted. Only a month ago it had been rough and muddy. Shortly before the lane reached the yard there was a field entrance to my right where cattle were grazing. The gate was shut, but seeing a strand of cord across the lane I thought they'd recently returned from the yard after milking and assumed the cord was to prevent the cattle from escaping down the lane. I stopped and untied the cord and had only driven a few feet when, to my horror, the concrete turned to jelly! Fortunately my rear wheels were still on the hard surface and I was able to reverse. As I was backing out of this terrible mess I could hear a raised voice coming from the yard.

A very red-faced Jerry Williams was soon beating on the side of my car calling me all the names under the sun.

"In God's name, why didn't you read the notice?" he demanded, then seeing me modified his language a little. Sure enough, I could now see a board at the side of the lane with the words 'WET CONCRETE' written on it in large red letters. How had I missed it?

The damage amounted to two deep ruts a few feet long. Jerry

grabbed a plank and together we managed to work it over the unset concrete. Seeing the lane return to normal with little harm done, Jerry cooled down. I felt like making a quick exit and said I could always come back another time, but by now Angela had arrived on the scene and invited me in.

Simon was a likeable teenager who'd inherited his mother's dark hair and his father's bright eyes. He also shared his mother's quiet intelligence and seemed much older than his years. I was impressed by his reasons for wanting to be Confirmed.

"You see, I want to get this right, Mr Longfield. I've given my Confirmation a lot of thought. I honestly feel I've got three choices. I can either live in a rapidly decaying world which has little time for God; I can drop out; or I can become a Christian and try in some way to improve the world of the future."

Simon continued. "I've been impressed by some of my friends at school. Quite a few of them are members of the Mill Chapel Youth Fellowship."

At this point Jerry got up from his chair and pulled a leaflet out of the kitchen drawer. It announced the forthcoming visit of an American by the name of Jonas Young. He knew it was organised by the chapel folk and he wanted to know what I thought about it.

My reply was quite simple. "I've come across men training for the Anglican ministry thanks entirely to the Billy Graham missions in London. I think the Chapel Mill meeting will be similar. Whilst I'm wary of any kind of pressure or emotionalism that might lead to false decisions, clearly it works for some and I'm in no position to condemn it. As a matter of fact I'm thinking of going to the meeting myself. Why don't you come along."

*   *   *

I didn't say anything to the Williams family that evening, but it was quite a coincidence that Jerry had shown me the leaflet about Jonas Young because I was expecting a visit from Harold Deane the following day to talk about that very subject.

As I drove along the lane I recalled how Harold had taken over a defunct chapel in Westaleigh and brought it back to life. It was no secret that the Mill Chapel was packed on a Sunday morning with a congregation that would be the envy of any parish church. The Westaleigh parishioners hated Mill Chapel and had nicknamed its preacher 'Holy Harold'.

'The man's a menace'. 'He's a narrow minded bigot'. 'He thinks we're not good enough for him'. 'A hypocrite of the first order'. 'He preys on our congregation'. These were just a few of the compliments paid to 'Holy Harold'.

Charles Gold, the previous vicar, had described him as an ignorant fundamentalist, a dangerous man setting himself up as some kind of self-styled preacher. He considered Harold a 'sheep stealer' because of the way he got nearly every child in the parish to go to his Mill Chapel Sunday School. While Charles struggled with a small congregation in a huge, cold church, this warm comfortable chapel in a picturesque setting was attracting more and more of the church's supporters.

More evidence came from Tom Short, Westaleigh's other church-warden.

"They chapel folks talks about us as if we'm a load of 'eathens. They says you can't get to 'eaven unless you've signed one of they pledge cards, or whatever 'tis they calls 'un. 'Tis all about drink. Every time they 'ave a service that Deane goes on and on 'bout 'un. 'E even made out poor old Mr Gold wasn't a proper Christian. Us don't mind they chapel folks so long as they keeps theyselves to theyselves and don't poach our people. But us don't care for that Deane and they cards of 'is."

*   *   *

Harold Deane sat in our kitchen looking slightly uncomfortable. He was going on and on about the good hay season farmers were enjoying, but I knew this was not the purpose of his visit. To start the ball rolling I asked him about the pledge cards used at Mill Chapel.

Harold explained they were nothing to do with alcohol or being teetotal, they were simply cards recording a person's 'Decision for Christ' based on those used by Billy Graham. "Do you approve of Billy Graham?" At last Harold was getting round to the real reason for his visit.

I chose my words carefully. "I know for certain of two people whose lives have been changed by him. I used to be very sceptical about the Billy Graham missions, but now . . ."

Harold interrupted me. "Well, Mr Longfield, I'm sure you know I serve on a district committee which organises outreach meetings. We always look for support from local churches. The parish hall here at Ashenridge has been booked for a visit by Jonas Young. He's an American, an ex-gangster. I promise you he has an amazing story to tell of his conversion to Christianity. Will you support the evening and encourage others to come?"

I told Harold I would certainly come to the meeting, and I'd be happy to announce it at Ashenridge, but in view of past events at Westaleigh I decided to let them make up their own minds.

Rightly or wrongly I was not in favour of extended appeals or any form of emotionalism, so before Harold left I asked him how the service would end.

"With a hymn and a *short* appeal," he replied.

*   *   *

Stepping inside Ashenridge parish hall that evening was like stepping into another world. At least a hundred people were gathered, people of all ages. I was surprised at the number of teenagers there, a generation the church was failing to attract.

Harold came over and introduced me to a beaming Jonas Young. He wasn't a bit what I'd expected. Small, slightly built, almost insignificant. Was I really shaking hands with an ex-gangster?

At seven o'clock on the dot we were called to order and I was left to scramble for a seat at the back of the hall.

The service began with notices read by Harold. A middle-aged man, whom I didn't recognise, gave testimony as to how he'd become a Christian. The force with which we sung 'The Old Rugged Cross' must have been heard for miles around. Two members read from the Bible followed by Harold's reading from the Prodigal Son. All eyes were now fixed on Jonas. Harold's introduction was lighthearted enough, but the look on Jonas's face as he came to the front of the stage was deadly serious.

"My dear friends," Jonas spread his arms wide as if to encompass everyone. "My dear friends, I'm going to tell you a story now that you'll maybe find hard to believe. Picture a slum, an American slum in the 1920s. A young boy, abandoned by his parents, crouching in the gutter. Hungry, ill, weeping because nobody cared whether he lived or died."

He must have told his story hundreds of times, but it was still impressive.

Jonas's voice was getting louder and louder. He came to the very edge of the stage and staring at the audience cried, "Can you imagine what it felt like?"

You could have heard a pin drop. This was riveting stuff. Jerry and Angela Williams had decided to go to the meeting and Simon was sitting with them. The Waterheads were there, bottle-throwing Mabel hanging on every word.

"I turned bitter, I hated everyone. I was only a teenager when I got involved with a group of gangsters. Yeah, I got involved in all sorts of rotten crimes *and* I witnessed a murder. As the years went on I got harder and harder, I drank enough alcohol to sink a ship. Violence became my password. One evening, half crazed with bourbon, I found myself in a Christian coffee bar in New York. People were good there. They befriended me. An' I was doin' fine until I thought I recognised a girl who'd let me down. I went crazy and smashed the place.

Next thing I know I'm waking up in hospital, my head and hands covered in bandages. I didn't care if I lived or died. But there they were, the guys from the coffee bar, there at my bedside. They wouldn't give up on me and for the first time in my life I knew I was surrounded by good people, people who really cared about me.

It was 1957 and I didn't know it but my life was about to change forever. My friends invited me to Billy Graham's New York Crusade. At first I laughed at them. Me, Jonas Young, listening to a preacher man? Thank God they persevered. There were thousands in Madison Square Garden that day and I can still hear Billy Graham's voice preaching his simple Christian doctrine – salvation through faith in Jesus. He's the greatest Evangelist of the century. He's led thousands of people to make personal decisions to accept Jesus Christ into their lives, and I thank God I'm one of them."

If only the meeting had been left there it might have had a powerful and lasting effect, but Harold chose that moment to come back on stage. He spent a good ten minutes summing up what Jonas had said, then built up to an appeal for people to come forward and accept Jesus into their lives.

We sang a hymn 'Just As I Am', repeating each verse over and over again. Between each verse Harold made another appeal until, perhaps out of pity, one person had the courage to go forward. That person was Mabel Waterhead!

From being clearly moved by Jonas' words, Angela Williams now left the hall looking embarrassed and her husband went home an angry man.

His promise to end the meeting with a 'hymn and a short appeal' had obviously been forgotten. When I reminded him about it some days later he was unapologetic claiming God had led him to act as he did.

*   *   *

In the months following the mission Jerry and I got on well enough, but he shut up like a clam regarding his faith.

Simon Williams was Confirmed, and although it had been my fervent hope he'd remain a regular worshipper at Westaleigh Church, encouraging others of his generation to come along, he wanted to enjoy fellowship with like-minded people of his own age and joined the mid-week Mill Chapel. Sadly, the parishioners at Westaleigh could not accept his decision and condemned him.

Chapter 14

Making A Name

Snapdragons of all shades, scarlet and crimson sweet Williams, flaming red hot pokers and pungent tiger lilies transformed one corner of Westaleigh village into that glory which is forever England. Deep-blue delphiniums, tall hollyhocks, gentle granny's bonnets, these and many more filled every corner of this old-world garden.

Behind this riot of colour stood Walter Hagley's cream-coloured cottage, its tiny brown-framed windows peeping out of walls covered with honeysuckle and climbing roses. An ever-burning log fire sent wisps of blue smoke out of the tall chimney standing high over the steep thatched roof. By day the garden would hum with bees, in the evenings the air filled with the heady scent of hundreds of plants.

In springtime masses of bulbs grew there. Later in the year would come roses, sweet peas, golden rod and chrysanthemums. The greatest time in Walter's garden was late May and June. The occasional Whitsun tourist might find himself travelling down the narrow lanes round Westaleigh, dwarfed by high hedges, then Honeysuckle Cottage with its beautiful garden would suddenly spring into view.

Passers-by would stop their cars to admire Walter's pride and joy. He loved talking to them and showing them round the garden. Then it would be his wife, Elsie's, turn to appear and offer a cup of tea. Her guests would watch fascinated as she drew water by means of a handy-maid from the large hanging kettle that was always boiling over the smoking hearth.

Years ago the spot in front of Walter's cottage had been a village pond. Then it became an eyesore, a mass of nettles and brambles. When Squire Pollard died his Westaleigh estate was sold and Walter, his head gardener, had to move and content himself with becoming a farm labourer. The mess outside his new home offended his professional eye, so he appealed to Ben Barker, chairman of the parish council, who agreed to let him tidy it up and plant flowers there on the understanding that it remained parish land.

Since retiring, Walter spent most of his time in this garden. He also took over several other small unwanted plots belonging to various cottages in the village. There was no telling where he'd turn up. But it was always on the parish land in front of his cottage that Walter grew his best blooms. The soil where the old pond had once been was very rich. Perhaps that was why he won so many cups at local flower shows.

* * *

Things might have continued like this as Walter gloried in the golden autumn of his life, but disaster struck one September when Ben Barker died. In a battle to carry in the last of his straw before rain set in, Ben had suffered a fatal heart attack.

The parish council now needed a new chairman and it was here that Alfred McRoberts stepped in. A medium-built man with a distinctive Midlands accent, Alfred was full of drive and enthusiasm. It was assumed he had retired young, leaving a thriving biscuit factory behind him. Later it transpired the factory had fallen on hard times and he was lucky to have been bought out at a fair price. It was a great sadness to him that 'McRoberts Biscuits' was no longer a household name.

Alfred came to Westaleigh in 1955. He and his wife were in church on their first Sunday there. Soon Alfred was on the church council and his wife ran the flower rota. It was not long before he presented the church with a new lectern Bible. At his suggestion comfortable kneelers, a visitor's book and other items appeared in church, all largely financed by himself. He also donated a wooden seat which sat on a patch of grass outside the churchyard gate.

In 1956, following the death of Charles Palfreyman, there was need for a new churchwarden. Alfred was the obvious choice from the small congregation. Within a matter of weeks he had succeeded in riding roughshod over a one-hundred-year-old dispute about an ancient track that ran between the old and new churchyards. He stood up for the farmer who claimed he had a right of way for vehicles. The result was that during the winter months mourners had to struggle over thick muddy tracks to reach the graves. This led to another row with the vicar and church council, which by now included the formidable Sir William Radlett. Finding he was not getting his own way, Alfred promptly resigned and Sir William took over his post.

If Alfred found himself less than popular with the church council he was, of course, a hero in the eyes of the farmer. He was also popular with others, especially anyone with a grudge against my predecessor, the rather strict Charles Gold. On a wave of popular support he found himself voted on to the parish council, then on the sudden death of Ben Barker, became chairman. His undoubted drive and leadership made him the obvious person to take over.

With his enthusiasm and forcefulness Alfred soon woke up a rather sleepy council. Within a year the last few farms without mains had electric light. The Water Board at last took action and all the houses who wanted it had piped water. Serious discussion was also under way about providing mains sewage. The village was sharply divided about whether or not they wanted street lights, but before any proper discussion had taken place they appeared almost overnight. One glared straight into Walter Hagley's cottage. He was furious about it, telling everyone it kept him awake at night and would be the end of his roses.

Having disposed of most of these tasks, Alfred now turned his attention to widening the village street. Agricultural machinery was getting bigger and so were the lorries delivering bulk goods to the farms. There had been chaos on more than one occasion. Several people were happy to surrender a couple of feet off their gardens providing the council rebuilt their boundary walls. All this would help, but a much wider passing place was needed and there was only one place for it – the site of the former village pond in front of Walter's cottage.

A parish meeting was called to make a decision about the widening scheme. It was Alfred's undoing. Those who had agreed to surrender a strip of their gardens became very upset when they discovered that more than 'just a couple of feet' would be required. The main battle, however, was over Walter's garden. People were angry at the prospect of losing their beauty spot and the distress it was causing Walter. The more he was pressed over the matter, the more heated Alfred became. He blustered on that Walter had no right to it. The meeting turned into a shouting match and Alfred stormed out of the hall saying it was time everyone grew up.

Within a few minutes news of what was said spread round the whole community. Walter had shut himself inside his home weeping. The village was unanimous in its rage. Next morning it was discovered that someone had embedded an axe in Alfred's wooden seat. Even worse, when Tom Short, the other churchwarden, went into the church, he found Alfred's lectern Bible lying on the floor, a few choice words scribbled inside.

Sir William rang me. Someone would have to have a chat with Alfred and he felt it should be me. I did not relish this task, but the following day I found myself sitting in the drawing-room at Grange Park trying hard to bring the conversation round to the purpose of my visit. I was surrounded by Alfred's collection of French clocks which marked each quarter of an hour in chorus. They had all chimed twice before I managed to mention Walter Hagley. Alfred's face fell. He wanted to dismiss Walter's reaction as a matter of no importance and none of my business. Then I told him what had happened to the seat and the Bible. A torrent of abuse was poured over my head and against everyone, the church and parish in general, and Walter in particular.

I was relieved when his wife brought in some coffee. She somehow managed to calm the situation and Alfred eventually conceded that his visit to Walter had been a bit of a disaster. His intention was to find out exactly what agreement Ben Barker had made with him over the use of the land. It was unfortunate that Walter had gone on about street lamps and roses. As Alfred saw it, Walter was avoiding the real issues. On the other hand it hardly helped matters when Alfred refused a cup of Elsie's tea

*   *   *

The following Sunday I found a somewhat subdued Alfred in church. The damaged seat was now being repaired, the offending words had been erased from the Bible. I was preaching about our Lord's prophecy of the fall of Jerusalem. Suddenly it took on a new relevance.

"The prophecy of Jesus came true. When the Romans sacked Jerusalem, literally not one stone was left standing on another. If you go back to Jerusalem today, you can see virtually no structure above ground that Jesus knew, no building, no memorial, no inscription. Search the land, and what is there? Jacob's well, the spot where Jesus is supposed to have been born and another where He died, and an inland sea where once He preached and healed. But Jesus did leave a memorial, and one which can never perish, on the hearts of men.

We live thousands of miles from Israel, but even here we still find that living memorial of Jesus today, in the lives of men and women in this parish, changed by His death and resurrection. What greater record can there be than that?"

As my sermon continued I became aware of the effect it was having on Alfred. He did not look at all happy as he left the church, but I felt it was better to let him slip away rather than engage him in small talk.

Not long after this a stroke severely curtailed Alfred's activities. He gave up the chairmanship of the parish council and no more was said about Walter Hagley's garden. But the damage had been done. Walter abandoned his beautiful garden and instead would sit at the cottage door dwelling on the iniquities of 'Thikky McRoberts'. Bindweed strangled the pea sticks, weeds took over from the snapdragons and rubbish began to appear amongst what was left of the delphiniums and lupins.

Within eighteen months Alfred was dead and his family moved away. He left behind a Bible, a repaired seat, mains water, a string

97

of controversial street lights, and a corner of Westaleigh overgrown with nettles and brambles, the beauty of which was now but a fond memory.

He also bequeathed a very generous amount of money. I knew he'd been planning to provide Westaleigh church with a set of oak pews to replace the rather uncomfortable Victorian pine seats. A plaque bearing his name would have reminded everyone who had given them. Instead, he gave instructions for the money to go to a local orphanage.

Alfred also left this note: 'If I am to be remembered, let it be in the lives of people I have helped, rather than in wood or stone'.

Chapter 15

No Smoke Without Fire

As I approached Ashenridge bus shelter one morning I could hear the usual voices chattering away. "The very moment 'is back is turned, in comes that man with the flat cap, and she's off with 'im in 'is little grey car."

"Disgusting I calls it," added another.

"Fancy someone like 'er. Poor man. Who'd of thought it?"

"'Tisn't true, they'm not like that," came the familiar voice of Kitty from the centre of her gathering in the bus shelter.

"No smoke without fire," another was saying.

At that point I was spotted and the topic quickly changed.

"'Tis they bus people. They says they'm going to stop our buses. Only us don't believe 'tis true. What does yer think, Parson?"

I knew Kitty had switched the conversation. What she was saying was news to me. So, too, was this man in the flat cap. Whatever was it all about?

Just now it would have to wait. I was more concerned about a letter from the bishop which had arrived that morning. It read like this: "My Dear Longfield, I have in mind a deacon for you whom I will be ordaining at Trinity. Meanwhile I am sending Dr Parnall to help you. He has some interesting ideas about rural ministry."

I wondered just what sort of curate he had in mind this time. Furthermore, the name 'Parnall' set alarm bells ringing. Although new to the diocese, he already had a reputation for creating chaos. Did the bishop really think he could help, or was he sending him to get him out of the way?

"Now look here," came the angry voice of Sir William Radlett. "When Westaleigh joined Ashenridge, you promised us a service every Sunday. You said we would never be closed and now this diocesan official tells me we may only be allowed one Sunday service a month and has the infernal cheek to say we'll be lucky if we don't find ourselves closed in a year or two. We trusted you, and now you've let us down. You must have known what was being planned behind our backs. I'm going straight to the bishop and demand we be left alone. I knew something like this would happen when we were forced to come under Ashenridge. I realise you'll deny all this, but there's no smoke without fire."

I'd no sooner put the phone down when the front door bell was pressed with unusual vigour. Another enraged churchwarden, Will Swift, stood on the doorstep. On his journey home in the Leighford bus the driver had been asking him in a very loud voice why I wanted to run a bus round the villages to collect all the people for Sunday worship. He said people were already nicknaming my rumoured plan the 'mobile God shop'!

Hard on Will's heels came Colonel Waters who had heard a similar tale from the Post Office. What on earth was going on? To cap it all, I then had a phone call from Steve Birchall, the Combe Peter church-warden. He was horrified at the prospect of the bishop closing down his church.

I was about to ring the bishop myself when an elderly man appeared at the front door eyeing me through tiny steel-rimmed glasses. He wore a light fawn corduroy jacket, grey trousers, and a deer stalker hat which held down an untidy tangle of grey hair. For some reason I was not surprised when he told me his name was Parnall.

I showed him into the study then dashed across the hallway to tell Will and Colonel Waters that if they could bear with me I'd be in touch with them a little later on.

My first meeting with Dr Parnall did not get off to a good start. As I thought, he had been talking to Sir William and to the bus company.

When I asked why he hadn't had the courtesy to talk things over with me first he replied that since I had received a letter from the bishop he saw no need for a preliminary meeting.

Eventually we agreed to hold a meeting two evenings later so that he could present his ideas to all three church councils. I braced myself for a stormy session.

I called on Annie Cook to let her know about the meeting. Her garden happened to run alongside the village street at a point where people stopped to chat. She, too, had overheard rumours about a man in a flat cap. By the way people were talking, she suspected his calls were to the rectory. She thought I ought to know. Infuriating though Annie could sometimes be, I actually valued her judgement. She was not a gossip and her timely tips often meant I called on families just when help was needed. We had a good laugh about the rectory visitor and I threatened to buy a flat cap. Just then too much was happening for me to give the mystery man a second thought.

*   *   *

Two evenings later Dr Parnall faced some thirty angry church councillors. Based on some successful experiments in Eastern England, he proposed that instead of having a poorly supported service in each church every Sunday, we all get together for one big service. Perhaps we could take it in turns going from church to church. A local company would be prepared to lay on a regular bus service. In other places where this had been tried it had proved to be a great success.

We were living in days when parishes found it impossible to keep their ancient buildings going. To close a few of the least important churches would ease the burden on small communities. In future the limited value of past legacies would no longer pay the clergy, and the people would never be able to afford it. Telephones and cars were changing life, so it seemed sensible to cut down on clergy where possible.

"Which church will he close?" came a loud whisper from one corner.

"I'm not going to Ashenridge. My family has always worshipped at Westaleigh. That's the last you'll see of me," muttered someone else. Others followed.

"Gran left £100 to our church."

"What about all the money the Church Commissioners have?"

Oblivious to these comments, Dr Parnall brought his talk to a climax. He was offering the churches a new beginning with much better services, far less expense and better use of time and manpower, and above all real hope for the future.

"How many people were originally attending the individual churches you mentioned?" I asked. He thought it was about half a dozen in each. Then, remembering one huge and remote Norfolk church which was in the middle of a field, he corrected it to three in some cases. He spoke warmly of having attended a recent joint service there and found no less than thirty people present. What a wonderful boost for the life of that church. What hope it gave everyone.

Looking at our own three churches I reckoned between twenty-five and thirty-five people attended Ashenridge each week. As yet it was still only 8 plus a choir of 3 at Westaleigh. Combe Peter was growing quite fast with twelve at a normal service and on a good Sunday nearly thirty came to the new family services. Steve Birchall's pained expression showed how he would feel if they were expected to forego this service and travel elsewhere.

Dr Parnall seemed surprised by the figures I quoted and agreed that even twelve in a small church feels very different to 3 in a vast build-ing. He admitted that some of the churches he spoke of were not only huge but far away from villages. When pressed he also said that the joint church council meetings only worked when each church had a sub-committee to deal with its own repairs and local functions. So I asked whether instead of reducing meetings had they not just added another?

All round the room people were beginning to relax. What threatened to be a confrontation turned into a moderately helpful question and answer session. People began to appreciate something of the doctor's vision of parishes working together. There were certain things one small church on its own could never do, like youth work, or a more ambitious musical event. The churches working closely together here might come up with some wonderful ideas. There was no limit to what could be achieved.

*   *   *

Next morning I was in the middle of writing a letter to the bishop to sum up our meeting with Dr Parnall when I suddenly realised I was late for my weekly assembly at Ashenridge school. As I shot off I passed a small grey car driven by a man wearing a flat cap!

I remembered what Annie had said and my heart turned to stone. Mary? My dearest Mary. It couldn't be. Had I been so blind? I suddenly realised that Mary, whose hand could normally be seen everywhere in our home, had seemed less interested recently. Something was going wrong. What about that mysterious trip to town last Saturday? She just went off and only came back in time to cook a late lunch. She loved the children. She loved me, didn't she? There must be an innocent explanation.

At school that day I struggled through Joseph's dreams and the Feeding of the Five Thousand. Next I visited a patient at Combe Peter Isolation Hospital, then drove home, dreading what I'd find. Sure enough the house was empty. Mary had not even left a note. I walked round the garden. I attempted to write to the bishop yet again. Then for some reason I caught sight of an entry in my diary 'Art Class at Leighford'. Of course, that was it. One of Mary's tutors gave her a lift every Thursday to the art class. He must be the man in the flat cap. What a fool I'd been!

*   *   *

Mary laughed as I poured out my fears later that evening. But when I asked her if she was happy she seemed evasive and passed it off by saying that one day she *might* drive off into the sunset with a handsome man in a flat cap. Was there, I wondered, a grain of truth in this?

A day or two later I was passing Annie's hedge when she called out, "It's that man in the flat cap. He's getting more cheeky now. Last night he got out of his car and went into the church. When he came out again he met Peter Eastridge and started asking all sorts of questions. I thought you ought to know."

Could it possibly be the same man? He certainly drove a small grey car *and* wore a flat cap. There was plenty of smoke, but what about the fire?

Chapter 16

Nightmares

The warm fruity voice of Mrs Batchelor was on the other end of the phone. She was so excited she could hardly get her words out. She wanted both of us to join her for a coffee and all would be revealed when we met.

Alarm bells began to ring. What was she planning this time? Did she have another outrageous idea for the church, or did she want to get us involved in another charity event? It so happened I had to visit an elderly patient at the hospital and couldn't get to the coffee morning and Mary volunteered to go on her own.

∗   ∗   ∗

A day or two later Steve Birchall rang me. He was a little concerned about a grey car that kept appearing in Combe Peter village. One day it was parked by the church gates and that very morning it was there again.

Somewhat disturbed by this news I felt it was time to clear things up with Mary. It must be the art tutor who met her on Thursdays. I was just about to broach the subject when the door bell rang and a young man wearing a flat cap stood on the doorstep. Parked on the drive behind him was a slightly battered grey Austin. He seemed most surprised when, rather ungraciously, I asked, "I suppose you're looking for my wife?"

"Actually I came to see you, sir," he said. "I believe the bishop wrote

105

to you about me. I'm Roy Edwards." For a moment the name meant nothing to me. Then I recalled the reference in the bishop's letter to someone being ordained on Trinity Sunday who might possibly become my curate.

I could have hugged him. My fears about Mary vanished as he explained that he and his wife, Lucy, had decided to spend a few days in the West Country and although he'd called at the rectory a few times he could never find anyone at home. He and Lucy had taken the opportunity to visit Ashenridge Church and had visited the other parishes as well.

If first impressions were anything to go by Roy seemed ideal, and I hoped that he would prove suitable for the job. He accepted my invitation to come round for a meal that evening so we could talk things through.

*   *   *

Roy's appearance that afternoon was very well timed. I was supposed to be interviewed at the local Women's Institute that evening about my life as a rector, but I asked Mary if she would talk to the WI instead about her role as a clergyman's wife as she was going to the meeting anyway.

Mary looked daggers at me. "And I suppose you want me to lay on a meal for your guest as well? I seem to spend most of my time feeding unexpected visitors. It was half the choir last week. Now someone else turns up out of the blue and . . ." Mary's voice tailed off as two hungry children arrived home from school.

Roy had both feet placed firmly on the ground. He and his wife were country folk through and through. It soon became clear that he shared my vision of bringing new hope and purpose back into sleepy country churches.

Unlike his contemporaries, he did not see his future as a curate in some large urban church. He was keen to be trained for rural ministry. He looked forward to the experience he would get by working in the villages. Once he got himself established, he would love to run a Bible study group and to reinvigorate Sunday schools and youth work. He had ideas about joint events and house parties for all the parishes. His wife could run choirs and train people to play guitars in church, and so on.

As we ate our meal it became obvious we shared many of the same goals for rural parishes, but when he remarked that the Mothers' Union was not for him I could see Mary frowning. She was soon smiling again when he enthused about gardening and shared her interest in painting. He would also be happy to take Sunday School off her hands.

Mary looked quite relieved when it was time for her to go to the WI. With the help of the children we washed up and Roy made his way home. By the time Mary returned we both felt so tired we fell into bed without saying a word.

*   *   *

The next day, after visiting the school and the Isolation Hospital, I spent a lot of time in the garden. I prepared the ground for the spring tilling and burnt loads of rubbish from the previous year. A pile of branches from an overgrown hedge gave me just what I needed to get a good fire going.

At tea I proudly told Mary about all my efforts while she'd been out. Instead of being pleased she exploded. Did I not realise that those branches were being saved for next year's pea sticks? Why couldn't I stick to my part of the garden without interfering with hers? Did I ever listen to what she was saying?

At that moment the telephone rang. Mrs Batchelor sounded like an excited mother about to announce the arrival of Father Christmas at a children's party. She had something to show me. She knew how delighted I'd be. She could not tell me now, but if I came to the church at about eleven o'clock tomorrow she'd be ready.

A wedding interview took me straight out after the phone call and by the time I got back Mary was in bed fast asleep.

*   *   *

"Now open your eyes and look," said a beaming Mrs Batchelor, leading me into Ashenridge Church. "What do you think of that? Don't you think it makes the church feel warm and comfortable?"

To my horror bright red curtains hung from several windows. Unfinished and with untidy ends top and bottom, they made the church look more like a lounge. The colour screamed against the maroon carpeting in the choir stall.

Before I could say anything Mrs Batchelor spoke again. "No, don't worry, Mr Longfield, I realise they're not finished. Your wife thought they were marvellous. We just want to know if you would like them put square in front of the windows like this, or cut to shape and put inside the individual arches? We want to get them finished by Easter. Do say you like them. We've got enough to do one for each window, and some for your vestry as well."

She was so thoughtful, so kind. I didn't want to offend her, but I explained I had to put it to the church council and then get diocesan approval. I added that we had to be careful in choosing the correct liturgical colours, and we would need to take expert advice.

Mrs Batchelor looked disappointed, then she cheered up and said, "If it is the wrong shade of red, I'm sure we can dye them. I just want to have a lovely church that everyone can enjoy."

I was angry with Mary for encouraging Mrs Batchelor. She'd said nothing to me about it and really dropped me in the soup. When I got back to the rectory there was no sign of Mary and I remembered she'd gone to London with her tutor to see an art exhibition.

I stepped into the church for peace and consolation, but was denied even this. There was Len, keen to tell me he'd only paid a shilling at Leighford over-sixties jumble sale for yet another new jacket. He was about to launch into a list of all his other sale purchases, but as he paused to take breath I jumped in to remind him of his promise to fix the porch light.

That brought Len on to another subject. He thought it would be a wonderful idea to have a 'Gloomy Air' at Ashenridge Church. Past experience taught me to make sure I knew what Len was talking about before agreeing with him, so I asked him what he meant.

"Well, 'tis like this. I seed it down to cousin Tom's church. 'Tis all done with bright lights."

"Oh, you mean floodlighting?"

"Well sir, I do and I don't, leastways not what you'm thinkin'. You see, they lights up the tower, but they does it from the hinside. Only you see they uses coloured lights all over. That's what they calls it, 'Gloomy Airs'."

Were people going crazy? First Mrs Batchelor with her bright red curtains, now Len wanting coloured lights. All we wanted was for someone to suggest roundabouts and we could turn the church into a funfair.

"Len," I said. "Do you really think it would be suitable for our church? I know we need to get up to date, but isn't this taking things a bit far? Incidentally, why do you call it Gloomy?"

"Well they say the bishop liked it. Blessed it 'e did. 'E thought 'twas proper like. Tom says 'e wouldn't 'ave missed it for nort. Went on a whole week it did. Look, there's something about it in 'ere."

With that he delved deep into his pocket and out came a crumpled sheet of paper announcing a Son et Lumière at Badgermouth Church.

"Oh Len, now I know what you mean. It's a Son et Lumière."

"That's what I said, 'Gloomy Airs'."

*　　*　　*

The following afternoon I had a long chat with Colonel and Mrs Waters. They both agreed the curtains were inappropriate. Nobody wanted to offend Mrs Batchelor or drive her from the church, but to bring the matter up at the church council, of which she was a member, would be to court disaster. One or two people would be sure to speak their minds. Fortunately that meeting was a few days ahead and gave us a chance to act. Meanwhile, we needed to persuade Mrs Batchelor to keep quiet about her idea.

At tea-time Ann thoroughly enjoyed being 'Mum'. She made sure we left everything tidy afterwards. Both children promised to go to bed at their usual time and my evening was taken up with a village hall committee meeting.

I had only been home a couple of minutes when the phone rang. It was one of Mary's fellow art students with a message that the exhibition was so good Mary had decided to stay on in London. She'd tried ringing me but when she couldn't get an answer asked her friend to ring. I'd just got over the worries about the man in the flat cap. Now Mary's friend proceeded to tell me about their brilliant tutor. Since losing his wife he'd thrown everything into his painting. He was kindness itself with time to listen to everyone. It was thanks to his patience and gentle encouragement that his students were so happy and doing so well. He was Constable, Turner and Van Gogh rolled into one!

I had a very disturbed night. I dreamt of Mary leaving me, her angry face glaring reproachfully at me again and again, accusing me of all the things I'd done to annoy her – leaving her to deal with difficult people, demanding meals at short notice for unexpected guests, burning pea sticks. I saw an empty chair at mealtimes, a cold bed at night, weeping children abandoned by their mother, shocked parishioners, and that blasted man in a flat cap driving off with my wife into the sunset. The images came again and again in one terrible nightmare.

I paced round the room. I went downstairs and made a cup of tea. Where was Mary? Was she staying with her sister? I could ring in the morning, but if she wasn't there her sister would start asking all sorts of awkward questions. Was Mary in a hotel? Was she with him? She couldn't be. I didn't know what to believe any more.

At last daybreak came. During breakfast Ann, who was becoming a bit of a rebel, sensed all was not well and went out of her way to be nice to me. I felt we were drawing closer together, but neither of us mentioned Mary.

*   *   *

Some people find it hard to keep a secret and the suggestion that Mrs Batchelor kept her red curtains a surprise made her all the more keen to tell others. I was brought back to reality by a total of six phone calls that day from various members of the church council. One caller thought they would be 'really nice', three others were horrified and wanted to know why nothing had been said until now. Two more threatened to resign if the curtains ever appeared in the church.

Once again I called on Colonel and Mrs Waters and between us we came up with an idea. Instead of curtaining the windows, why not use them to create a partition at the back of the church. Perfect for Sunday School; ideal for meetings and socialising after a service. To everyone's relief Mrs Batchelor liked this idea and life at Ashenridge Church was back to normal, at least for the time being.

*   *   *

Mary returned home later that evening. Long after the children were in bed we talked. Life had become so hectic that any form of conversation had become a rare event and we'd got out of the habit of listening to each other. Mary confessed she had gone out with her tutor, but only because he was such a good listener. There was nothing in it.

I'd allowed parish life to take over. It was my fault that our family life had suffered. I made a solemn and loving promise to Mary it wouldn't happen again.

Inevitably, we got round to the subject of 'those red curtains'. Mary explained that over coffee Mrs Batchelor had simply produced the curtains for her to admire and had never indicated where she was intending to hang them.

As we settled down for the night it was good to hear Mary chuckling as I told her about 'Gloomy Airs' and Len's grand design to illuminate the church from the 'hinside'.

I fell into a deep sleep. At last, the nightmare was over!

Chapter 17

What Do You Fellows Do With Yourselves All Day?

It was my birthday and Mary was taking me out for a meal. On a quiet spring evening we left Betty Mansell in charge of the children and headed for the Poacher's Inn. Perched on a scenic bend in the Badger Valley we listened to the rush of the river and gazed at the lights of the inn reflected in the water.

Despite hoping to be alone for a few hours, we came across a very affable Jim Stillman standing at the bar. Although he could be cynical about the church, we always got on well together. He joined us for a drink and in the course of conversation jokingly asked, "What do you fellows do with yourselves all day?"

I threw the question back at him. "What do you think?"

He stopped for a moment then ticked a list off on one hand. Sunday services, the odd funeral, wedding or baptism, and cups of tea with old ladies. I laughed and we let it go at that.

If I'd told Jim what was in my diary for the next day he would have smiled, stroked his chin and dismissed my job 'for what it's worth'. There were only two entries – 10.00am funeral, 7.30pm Westaleigh Church Council.

*   *   *

Life, however, was never as simple as that, especially where Westaleigh was concerned, and looking at my diary reminded me of the previous church council meeting.

How different things might have been if Wilfred Thomas had exercised a little more patience when presenting his ideas. He'd moved to Westaleigh from Bristol and had quickly become a regular worshipper. When the secretary to the church council resigned because of failing eyesight, Wilfred was asked to replace her.

People were delighted to learn he was writing a history of the village, and agreed that the sale of his greetings cards featuring the church and churchyard would raise some much-needed funds.

Then came the bombshell. To bring new life to the church Wilfred proposed we serve coffee and biscuits after the morning service. It had worked a treat in Bristol, giving the congregation a chance to mix socially rather than rush off after the service. It sounded like a good idea to me, but I wanted Wilfred to take things slowly and remember that to the older generation the very thought of eating or drinking in church, other than taking Communion, was regarded as sacrilege.

The church council members were thunderstruck. "Sacrilege! That's the only word I can think of to describe it. Sacrilege!" Mrs Mock had cried in horror at that meeting two months ago, her three chins wobbling like the enormous jellies she made for the over-sixties club.

Some said they would never come to the church again if it were reduced to some sort of café. Tom Short chipped in saying this was the sort of irreverence that went on at that terrible Mill Chapel. Mrs Mock was adamant the cleaning ladies would resign. Confetti was one thing, coffee stains and biscuit crumbs quite another.

*   *   *

I found myself wondering whether it might be better to let most of Westaleigh Church Council resign. These old reactionaries, who seemed devoted to ancient buildings and the past, were a complete barrier to new life. Simon Williams had been condemned by them for joining the Mill Chapel Youth Fellowship. Wilfred Thomas might well suffer the same fate.

Then I read in the Bible that Jesus in His ministry did not break a bruised reed or quench smoking embers of faith. I remembered how the once negative parishioners at Combe Peter had changed. Today, with faith rekindled, they were less afraid to adapt and we were seeing the congregation grow. Somehow Westaleigh needed motivating in the same way.

My thoughts brought me back to what lay ahead that day. I had to face up to Westaleigh Church Council that evening so I knew it was vital I get hold of Wilfred Thomas and read his minutes beforehand. Unfortunately, he must have left home early as there was no reply when I phoned. That meant I must slip round to see him when he came home for lunch.

There was no gathering after the funeral so I just had time to look in on a new family before going to see Wilfred at lunch time.

*　　*　　*

Janice Low was a harassed-looking young mum. My visit proved just the occasion for her to pour out all her troubles. Any thoughts of getting hold of the minutes before the meeting were fading.

Janice told me her husband was still in bed, very depressed. He'd lost his job and the debts were piling up. Their youngest child was ill with a suspected ear infection, and Janice didn't know how she'd get him to the surgery. I had no alternative but to offer to take them in my car. I still hoped I could catch Wilfred before he returned to his office.

We waited for over half an hour at the surgery and the prescription had to be picked up before the chemist closed for lunch. On our way back I saw Wilfred, driving in the opposite direction.

A hasty lunch of bread and cheese was followed by a home visit to one of my parishioners who was very poorly and had asked if I'd give her Communion. Ironically, at this little service I found myself reading these words: 'Be still and know that I am God'. That service was an oasis of peace in a hectic day.

*　　*　　*

Returning home I was surprised to find a brown bundle on the study table.

"I'm sorry," Mary said. "You were in such a hurry at lunch-time I forgot to tell you, Wilfred brought it. He can't get to the meeting tonight and sends his apologies."

The minutes were as I'd feared: 'The proposal to serve cups of coffee after morning service was rejected by Mrs Mock who without even considering it stated it was a sacreligious idea. Equally unhelpful statements were made by four other members. The resolution was dismissed before anyone had a chance to consider it'.

There was only one thing for it. I'd have to cut a page out of the minutes book and substitute my own version. At least I could look forward to a peaceful meeting.

*　　*　　*

Janice Low had called me back again. The solicitors had been in touch about their bad debts and they were about to lose everything. Phil just didn't seem to understand the seriousness of it all and was driving Janice mad fiddling with those 'silly little bits of paper'.

He was still in bed, casually leafing through a stamp collecting magazine. He saw me glancing at it and before we knew it we were in a world of Penny Blacks and Twopenny Blues. He showed me his collection, and being a collector myself, I immediately spotted the Victorian Penny Reds. He had at least three copies of plate 225, quite a rare stamp. Those 'silly little bits of paper', as Janice called them, were worth a tidy sum, enough to pay off their debts and have plenty left over.

Phil started to relax and admitted he'd felt unable to cope. This gave me a golden opportunity to talk about people in the Bible who had gone through desperate times. Moses was one of them, yet after a long spell in the wilderness God called him by the burning bush to go back and serve Him in a new way.

115

Any hopes of a peaceful meeting were dashed when Mrs Mock declared: "I want to make it quite clear, if there are going to be cups of coffee in church, I shall not be cleaning, nor will I attend services."

"Nor will I," echoed other voices.

Disliking their threatening tone I waded in. "I'm aware that at our last meeting this matter was broached in a rather unfortunate manner. Wilfred can't be with us this evening, but surely we can talk things over as friends."

I could see one or two people were thinking of leaving, but I hadn't finished.

"Again and again I've heard you say 'Why do we have to do all the work . . . why can't some of the youngsters take their share?' Wilfred joined our committee full of new ideas and enthusiasm, so I ask you to treat him kindly. Don't be in a hurry to dismiss his ideas, think about the principles that lie behind them."

"If the rector wants us to resign, then we will," retorted Mrs Mock, making as if to leave the room.

"Before you go, Mrs Mock, I'd like to thank you for all you've done. I appreciate the fact you've attended this church all your life, and that you and your husband have given tremendous support. Your life of service to the community has been second to none."

Mrs Mock's chins wobbled in all directions as she flopped back in her chair.

"I've called late at your house and found you busy making jellies and cakes for endless parties. I wonder how many tasks you've performed and nobody's even noticed. I know that after Christmas you spent the best part of three days getting rid of the candle grease that was accidentally spilt during the carol service. Through thick and thin, through family sadnesses and traumas, you've carried on. Not unreasonably many of you complain that the younger generation are fickle, unreliable. But think how much you have to teach them. I'm truly sorry if you decide to leave us."

Mrs Mock remained silent for a few seconds, then turning to her friends and addressing me at the same time she said, "Well, I suppose that puts things in a different light. I'm sorry if I was a bit hasty, Mr Longfield. Perhaps we've all been a bit hasty."

I breathed a sigh of relief and the rest of the meeting went off without a hitch, but I still had one hurdle to cross. I must tell Wilfred why I'd doctored his minutes.

*   *   *

The clock in my study was chiming ten when I got home and a mountain of paperwork on my desk needed attention. But I was exhausted and simply wanted to get to bed.

Mary saw me glance at my diary for the following day. Once again there were just two entries – 11.00am Charity meeting, 7.30pm Confirmation class. A mischievous grin spread across her face as she asked me, "What do you fellows do with yourselves all day?"

Chapter 18

If Only People Would Listen

Desmond stood alone in the middle of Ashenridge school playground. A lanky, rather sullen looking ten year old with coarse brown curly hair, he always wore his older brother's cast-offs, shabby grey shirts that were far too big for him, and equally large black trousers with holes in them. He and his family were new to the village, and the way the other children ignored him confirmed comments we'd heard from Paul and Ann that he was very unpopular.

Ashenridge was a state school but I was welcomed there from the start. Jack Beam, the headmaster, was an interesting man. He'd come to Ashenridge with some evacuee children during the war and stayed on at the school long after the original children returned to London. Eventually he became the head. His early experiences in tough inner city schools tended to make him less than sympathetic with the odd problem child.

"He's a funny lad," Jack said. We were discussing Desmond over a cup of tea in the staff room during break: "We can't get him to work, he's sullen and a poor mixer. A bit crafty though, and can be a ringleader when there's trouble. No good at football either, more's the pity."

"But he's new here, isn't he? Perhaps he hasn't adjusted yet from his last school? Does he need time to make friends?"

"Not a bit of it. I've seen it all before. I'm afraid he's got a nasty streak in him. That's why the others won't play with him."

A few days later I happened to be looking out of one of our back windows when I spotted a group of boys in the bushes being egged on by Desmond. They were aiming stones at the rectory. I shouted at them. The others fled in all directions, but I managed to chase Desmond back to his home.

His widowed mother told me she would sort him out, and offered to pay for any damages. "I can't make him out," she complained. "He's no good, he can't even kick a football properly. His brother Peter's so different. He passed his eleven-plus and now he's at the Grammar School. His teachers are very pleased with him. He's such a good boy and I just wish Desmond was like him."

*   *   *

The next morning I happened to look in at the school during break. This time Desmond was not on his own in the playground, but surrounded by a group of smaller boys.

"Desmond seems to be getting on better with the others now," I commented to Jack Beam.

"I don't think they like him very much," Jack replied. "I'll be glad when he leaves this school. I'm sorry to have to say it but he's a nasty piece of work."

That phrase 'a nasty piece of work' wouldn't go away, and by some strange coincidence that evening I found myself reading about another nasty piece of work in the New Testament called Zacchaeus, a tax collector who extorted money from the poor to spend on high living. But Jesus did not write him off. He spent time with him, and as a result Zacchaeus turned from being a thief into a benefactor. Desmond went on my prayer list straight away, not that I expected an instant miracle.

When I got home at teatime, Mary told me that just after the end of school she'd heard noises in the bushes at the back of the house. She went out to investigate and, sure enough, heard the sound of retreating feet. My investigation revealed two or three sets of small footprints and a set of larger ones.

Paul was very angry. They were disturbing birds' nests and other wild habitats which he'd been observing in the shrubberies near the house. I decided to lay a trap. At the back of the house were some old panes of glass, so Paul and I put these out in a prominent place not far from the bushes. Paul suggested I put some pieces of wood with them to make it look as though I were building a greenhouse. We hoped this might prove a tempting target.

*   *   *

Earlier that day I'd happened to meet my GP, Dr Ash, just as he was getting into his car between calls. In the course of conversation I mentioned Desmond.

"That young man just needs someone who'll listen to him," he said. "Just like I wish a certain lady in your parish would shut up and listen to me".

Mrs Loveband was one of the doctor's bugbears. She complained of being ill and went to see him regularly. All she wanted was pills and she flatly refused to see a specialist. I offered to have a chat with her and called round that afternoon.

"Come in, rector," she said, looking delighted to see me. "'Tis good to see you. Come in and us'll 'ave a cuppa tea."

Before I had a chance to ask her how she was feeling she started. "Funny thing, us was only thinkin' this mornin' when Mr Turner was at the rectory, what 'appy times us all 'ad." Fifteen minutes later I was still hearing about fêtes and concerts in years gone by and the promised 'cuppa' was nowhere in sight.

Seeing me gaze in the direction of the Rayburn, she put the kettle over the hot plate and it soon began to sing. Then she remembered the things she'd been making for the forthcoming local hospital fête. Proudly she displayed her handicrafts for me to admire: hand-knitted socks, stuffed cuddly toys and tea cosies. Each item had a story to go with it. Meanwhile the kettle was boiling its head off.

The hospital fête gave me the perfect chance to mention doctors. Unfortunately 'doctors' gave Mrs Loveband a marvellous chance to tell me all about the different doctors she'd known. It was three o'clock before she got round to making tea and I was still getting nowhere. One last ploy remained, the diseased looking cacti by the door. I said they looked as though they could do with some tender loving care. Mrs Loveband missed the point. "Oh, do you like 'em, rector? Us'll give you one or two to take 'ome." Mary could not stand cacti, but it would have been rude to refuse. Having failed in my mission, I now found myself hastening home carrying three miserable cactus plants. I felt very sorry for the doctor.

*   *   *

I added the three cacti in their pots to my trap. They helped to make the target look more convincing. I'd hardly crouched in position near the bushes before I heard the back gate open and in crept three boys. Suppressing nervous giggles, they hunted around under the bushes until each had gathered a collection of suitable stones. Then, egged on by Desmond, they advanced.

"Wow look at that," Desmond gasped, gazing at the pile of glass. "Let's help him put up his glasshouse!"

"Ssssh," said one of the others. "The old woman's over there."

"Don't be silly, it's only a bird in a tree," replied Desmond. "Don't be a chicken. Get those stones moving then hop it quick."

Desmond came forward in front of the others and threw the first stone. There was a sound of breaking glass. Just then the others saw me as I shot out from behind the bush.

"Look out," the others cried as they fled. Before realising I was there, Desmond's second stone was on its way. It missed the glass and hit one of the cacti for six.

A dazed Desmond found me holding him firmly by the collar. "It wasn't my fault," he lied. "The others made me do it. Everyone's against me."

"Can you blame them," I said. "If you go on like this what do you expect? I'm a good listener, you know. Why don't you tell me about your problems."

After a struggle Desmond began to tell his story. At home he was

121

made to feel stupid because his older brother was good at everything and got all the praise. While Desmond was expected to do all the chores, his brother was allowed to go upstairs to do his schoolwork. His mother wanted him to be a carbon copy of his older brother so it was hardly surprising that Desmond's life was not working out very happily. Even allowing for some exaggeration, from what I'd seen there was substance in what he said.

School was no better. According to Desmond, the headmaster had little use for boys who were neither good at work nor sport. While this might be an over-simplification, I did have some sympathy. After a pause he looked at me and said, "Now what are you going to do?"

Ignoring the question, I tried to find out what he really liked doing. He was keen on making things so I showed him a pile of wood in our garden shed and he said he'd like to have a go at making a garden gate.

Over the next few weeks Desmond came regularly to work in our garden. When it was wet he worked on the gate, and on dry days he tended a plot in the vegetable patch. Soon we had a freshly creosoted gate hanging in the garden and several rows of lettuces and carrots.

Impressed, I went round to have a chat with his mother. I invited her to come and see Desmond's achievements but she informed me she was too busy, and had great difficulty believing her younger son was capable of anything.

*   *   *

Quite unaccountably Desmond suddenly abandoned his good work. Bindweed began to choke the lettuces and chickweed smothered the carrots.

At school Desmond reverted to his sullen self and would shrink away if he happened to see me coming. At home he was more resentful and difficult than ever. Elsewhere he was another man, chief amongst his gang of outlaws. Unfortunately these outlaws did not confine themselves to the meadows and woodlands of old England. They felt that the church required their attention as well.

One Friday afternoon Mrs Pink went into church to arrange the flowers. She heard a scurrying of feet then noticed a rather strange smell. Initially Mrs Pink thought someone was smoking behind the font, then to her horror discovered a pile of smouldering hymn books.

Having dealt with the fire, Mrs Pink was on her way to ring the police when she happened to bump into me. I said I would prefer to deal with the matter myself and reluctantly she agreed to postpone her phone call.

Desmond was not at home. I eventually found him skulking in a farm shed not far from the church. He was alone, abandoned by the others. Even he realised he'd gone too far. The story he told me was rather what I'd expected.

As soon as it was known he was working in the rector's garden Desmond had been mocked for being a goody-goody. He confessed to planning the fire, but did it when he knew someone would be there to put it out. He also told me how his mother insisted he hand over the pocket money I'd given him for his work in the garden. She said he would only waste it, and in any case his hard working brother needed it more than he did as he was always studying and had no chance of earning anything himself.

I had a responsibility to tell Desmond's mother what had happened. When she knew there was a likelihood of the police being involved she became a little more approachable. I tried to persuade her to appreciate Desmond for what he was, not what she thought he ought to be, but within seconds she was praising Peter again.

I also called at the school and had a word with Jack Beam who promised to keep a fatherly eye on Desmond. Finally, I reassured Mrs Pink that it was exceedingly unlikely there would be a repetition of this petty arson. Although he never knew it, Desmond did the church a favour because he'd burnt the unsightly old books at the back of the church which nobody had the heart to throw away. The only real damage was a scorch mark on a small mat.

*   *   *

All this happened at a time when Roy Edwards, my first curate, and his wife, Lucy, had just joined us. To help with their garden I drove a young man over to them twice a week. Once he'd paid off his debt for the damage to the church mat we let his wages accrue. One day Roy took him out to buy a fishing rod and then taught him how to fish. They became good friends and in due course Desmond became an active member of Roy's youth group.

*　　*　　*

One September morning two presents were brought to our door. The smaller one was a very fine trout which Desmond had caught with his recently purchased rod.

The look of pride on his face said it all.

The larger present came in several crates which consisted of Mrs Loveband's entire collection of cacti. It turned out that the doctor had persuaded her to see a specialist who advised her she had a benign growth. As usual, she wouldn't listen when he reassured her she did *not* have a fatal disease and proceeded to make a will, choose her hymns, an undertaker and burial plot.

She was determined I should become the proud owner of her cacti collection before she died 'as you're so keen on them'.

Chapter 19

Things Are Not Always What They Seem

"I don't mind what I'm asked to do," Roy Edwards declared, "but I will not, definitely not, appear at a Mothers' Union meeting. It's nothing but a cosy club for grannies."

All I'd asked him to do was make a brief appearance and say a few words about himself, and the tone of his voice took me by surprise. He'd only been with me a few days since his ordination in June. The bishop warned me he was 'very evangelical with some cut-and-dried ideas'. The son of a headmaster of a country school, he'd read English at university intending to follow in his father's footsteps. A lifelong churchgoer, his faith was deepened and much influenced by a Billy Graham mission he attended. While working for his degree, he felt a calling to the Christian ministry, and against all advice by the diocese he chose to study at a very low church training college. So, the bishop had an ordinand on his hands whose churchmanship severely limited the parishes to which he could send him. Knowing his love of the countryside he sent him to me.

Before he arrived in Ashenridge I had already established that Roy was charming, reasonable, and far from the extremist my fellow clergy had labelled him. Like any young man straight from college he was full of idealism and enthusiasm, which is exactly what I expected of a man of twenty-seven. He was the sort of curate I'd been praying for.

*   *   *

At heart I knew there was an element of truth in Roy's opinion. Ever since the parish hall opened in 1935, three o'clock on the first Tuesday of each month was the sacrosanct hour when the MU met. The branch still proudly boasted several foundation members. To outsiders it may have looked like a cosy little society, and not everyone in it had the vision of Moses or the evangelistic drive of St Paul.

Roy's wife, Lucy, was also inaccurate when she referred to it as a 'Grandmothers' Union'. Mary belonged to it, and so did three others who still had children living at home. In fact, there was a much deeper reason why I respected the MU. In many small parishes its members formed the backbone of the church, dedicated people who kept everything going, not just by attending services and running bazaars but prepared to put time aside for others and to pray for the church and the people of the parish.

*   *   *

I fervently hoped Roy and Lucy would shed some of their preconceived ideas. As in previous years the September MU meeting took the form of a service in church instead of gathering in the hall. Unfortunately I was going to be away that day so, tongue in cheek, I asked Roy if he would be willing to conduct a week-day service for me.

"Of course," he said, and added cautiously, "Who will be coming to it?"

"The Mothers' Union," I replied.

"Oh well if it's in church that should be all right. Mind you, I still stand by what I said."

"And there's a cream tea afterwards. They always have the most wonderful scones and fruit cake," I added quickly.

"OK Jack, I promise I'll do my best."

"Bring Lucy, too," I ventured.

"That might be pushing things a bit too far," he chuckled.

*   *   *

Next morning I prayed that somehow Roy would get over his prejudices. If he wanted to continue in rural ministry he would almost certainly inherit a Mothers' Union somewhere. The answer to my prayer began in a strange way.

Shortly before the service Roy happened to call on Maud Cosway. Maud had been a member of the MU for many years and since the death of her husband the meeting was one of the highlights of her month. Roy asked Maud why she'd joined, what she got out of it, and whether it helped her in her Christian life.

"Oh yes, dear, we always have lovely times together and meet our friends. Of course many of those I remember are now gone, and the younger ones aren't the same. I always love my cup of tea and a chat. You see, dear, I can't get to church very much on Sundays, I cook for the family that day. The Mothers' Union is my little church. I really enjoy it."

"What do you think about the talks?" Roy enquired.

"Well, the ones I always look forward to most are the ones about flowers."

"Flowers of the Bible?" Roy asked, hopefully.

"On no, dear, flowers in our gardens for decorating the church."

"Don't you sometimes have speakers who talk about things like prayer?"

"Oh yes, but I don't find those so interesting."

Roy said nothing but came away fuming. So this was what the MU was like. It was just as he'd supposed. Now he had all the proof he needed to show it was nothing more than a comfortable club for old ladies. He grew more and more angry, but there was no way he could back out of the service since I was away, and in any case several members had told him how much they were looking forward to it.

Roy was not in a very good frame of mind when he arrived at the church. His mood was not helped when he was told he could not use the hymns he had chosen because they were not in the special MU service book. He then found to his horror that it was not the usual organist, but dear Mrs Tingle, who played hymns in half time!

Somehow Roy survived the service. Then came the real test. Mrs

Pearse, the enrolling member, said, "Ladies, I'm sure you'll agree how lovely it is to see Mr Edwards here this afternoon. We're so sorry his dear wife couldn't come because we know how much she would have enjoyed it. Thank you, Mr Edwards, for such a nice service. Perhaps you would kindly say grace before we have our cream tea."

Roy found the afternoon becoming more and more of a strain, and being introduced to Mathilda Pink proved to be the last straw. She was a formidable member of Ashenridge MU, did not suffer fools gladly, and certainly did not mince her words.

"I believe I saw your wife going into to town just after lunch. Why didn't she want to join us? We sent her an invitation. Some of us have not met her yet."

Roy tried to be polite and excuse Lucy by saying she had shopping she must do.

"So have I," retorted Mrs Pink. "But I can still manage to get here. I think it's a very poor show. A fine cleryman's wife she'll make."

This was too much for Roy. He said it was none of her business, told her a few home truths about the Mothers' Union, and stormed out. White faced and speechless, Mrs Pink collapsed into the arms of her friends, the top half of her mauve jacket covered in strawberry jam and cream, her matching hat crushed to one side of her head.

*　　*　　*

I'd only been back at the rectory a few minutes when Roy appeared on the doorstep looking distressed. He wanted to put me in the picture before others started complaining. I told him in no uncertain terms I was appalled at the way he'd behaved and it would be a very long time before he'd be invited to another MU meeting, which was probably music to his ears.

An angry Mathilda Pink rang later that evening to say she and her fellow members had found Mr Edwards' comments about a club for old ladies very hurtful and totally inappropriate. "After all, Mr Longfield, I'm only in my fifties."

I tried to explain that these days many of the younger clergy had a false impression of the MU and the only way to deal with the issue would be to prove it was untrue. A slightly calmer Mrs Pink said goodnight, but as I got ready for bed I couldn't help mulling things over and fell asleep wishing the problem would be gone by the morning.

An uneasy atmosphere hung over Ashenridge Church in the weeks that followed and there were one or two noticeable absentees at Harvest.

*   *   *

At our regular Monday meeting Roy came up with the strange story of an old couple who lived in a lonely cottage just off Ashenridge Moor. He'd often noticed a track leading into the woods, and one day his curiosity got the better of him. To his surprise he found himself standing outside a tumbledown cottage that looked as if it had been forgotten for many years. He thought he was dreaming when he saw an old woman inside the door wearing an apron made of sacks. A very thin, unshaven man was sitting inside gazing into a tiny flicker of fire in the huge hearth.

The Hartons made Roy welcome and asked him inside where he found himself sitting on the edge of a filthy chair with nasty-smelling stuffing spilling out of it. It seemed nobody ever came to see them, and their only weekly visitor was the oil man. Besides providing fuel for their lamps he occasionally brought them some tins of food. The old couple seemed so weak they hardly had the strength to make up the fire, let alone cook a meal. Yet on the table, amidst a jumble of plants, boxes, papers and snoring cat, Roy spotted the remains of a cooked meal on two tin plates.

He decided it was quite the worst place he had ever seen. It stank of mildew and decay. Chickens came running in and out of the open door. A pile of coal was stacked in one corner along with a rusty bicycle.

When Roy finished telling me his story I could hardly keep a straight face. Everybody in the parish knew how the old couple would play one person off against another. They had no close relatives, but I knew who looked after them. I suggested Roy pay a visit to Mrs Pearse who would be able to tell him more about it. I did not, however, remind him that Mrs Pearse was also the MU enrolling member.

*   *   *

Several days later Roy told me he'd been quite shaken to learn from Mrs Pearse that she and other members of the MU knew all about the Hartons and had been helping them for years. Sometimes it meant a three mile round walk from the village to deliver their shopping, and Mrs Pink organised a regular meal service. Nobody could persuade the couple to change their cleaning habits, but they were happy enough.

Mrs Pearse went on to tell Roy that the Mothers' Union had been running a 'good neighbours' scheme for years, backed by the Women's Institute and other well-meaning people. The Hartons were by no means the only ones who benefitted. What was more, the MU had a prayer group which always made a point of remembering people needing help. Roy was beginning to see another side to the Mothers' Union

*   *   *

Roy and Lucy gradually settled in at Westaleigh, but over one issue they totally disagreed. During his college vacations Roy had helped at a family centre in the East End of London. He was keen to give two or three of the children a holiday in the West Country. Lucy was horrified. Their home had just been decorated and their wedding money spent on nice carpets and good furniture. Did Roy want everything to be wrecked by a load of rough kids? Each time Roy broached the subject he received the same abrupt refusal.

Mathilda Pink had kept in touch with families in London she'd known during the blitz, and this year, thanks to the help of the MU, one of her dearest wishes was coming true. As a pilot scheme, six children from broken homes were coming from London to stay with adopted 'aunties' in the village for a long weekend. Nearly all of the MU members were involved in one way or another.

I knew that Roy and Lucy were going out that Saturday afternoon and would practically pass by the rectory so I asked them if they'd mind calling in. To their amazement they found our house and garden full of MU members. On the lawn six children from London were having a wonderful time playing with local youngsters while the MU members used our kitchen to prepare tea.

Before they had a chance to retreat from the scene a very enthusiastic Mrs Pearse proudly told Lucy and Roy all about this new idea. She was so pleased they had looked in.

Then a beaming Maud Cosway appeared carrying a heavy teapot. "How lovely to see you both. Sit down, my dears. You must have a cup of tea before you go."

As they were about to leave I noticed Roy and Lucy chatting with Mathilda Pink and overheard them saying they'd be glad to hear more about the scheme for another year. Mrs Pearse was promising to let Lucy have the necessary forms to join the Mothers' Union and said she would be made very welcome.

God certainly works in mysterious ways!

Chapter 20

An Open Book

"Rector, I want to know why nothing is being done about the disgraceful state of our churchyard," demanded a new member of Westaleigh Church Council.

It may have been a simple question, but it was enough to stir up strife yet again in Westaleigh. In fact I came to regret Roy and Lucy living in the vicarage there. I was hoping Roy's early days would be relatively calm yet he seemed to have started his ministry in the middle of a hornet's nest.

Nobody blamed Tom Short for the state of the churchyard. As well as having served half a lifetime as churchwarden, at seventy-one he still scythed as much of the grass as he could manage, and no one else volunteered to help him.

Many of the graves were buried under a riot of brambles and grass. During the summer most of the churchyard was carpeted with yellow buttercups, gorse and ragwort; in the evenings the rich scent of meadowsweet filled the air. As autumn approached luscious blackberries became ripe for the picking. Much of the churchyard remained like this from one year to the next, with one exception.

Just inside the main gate a narrow hand-clipped path turned off from the main track to the church. It then wandered off through deep undergrowth. Out of tangled grass and weeds peeped weeping cherubs and remnants of Victorian plaster wreaths covered by cracked glass domes. Anyone venturing along this path would eventually come across a beautifully-kept grave, it's shining white marble headstone simply engraved with the words 'in memory of Elias and Sophia Maythorn'. For thirty-five years they had lain there, yet their grave was tended as if their departure had been only yesterday.

Anyone visiting the churchyard on a Saturday afternoon might well come across the figure of a middle-aged lady wearing a straw hat, brim pulled down over her eyes. Emily Maythorn never missed her weekly visit. Even in the depths of winter, wearing the same straw hat, she would spend a good hour weeding and arranging flowers at her parents' grave. For Emily every grave told a story and she described each one as being like 'an open book'.

Emily sometimes attracted as big an audience on a sunny Saturday afternoon as Roy or I did for the Sunday service. Having trained as a nurse she'd hardly completed her course at the hospital than she was forced to return home to care for her ailing parents. After they died she was often called upon when anyone in the parish needed her help. Many of the people she'd once tended were now buried in this churchyard. She knew their life history, especially their illnesses, and often their last words. The villagers loved hearing her reminisce.

*   *   *

Emily never actually complained about the state of the churchyard because had it all been neatly mown it would have reduced the time she spent there and her chance of meeting people. She was not on the church council and, funerals apart, was never seen in church. She was probably unaware that at almost every church council meeting someone complained abut the state of the churchyard. Nor would she have known that every time the idea of buying a machine to do the job came up, Tom Short would object claiming, "Parson Bridges'd never 'ave a thing like that in 'yere. When I was a lad I once took a wheelbarrow through the churchyard and Parson Bridges almost 'excomm . . . excommu . . . excommunicated me for disturbin' the dead."

This command by the autocratic and long dead Parson Bridges needed challenging. I began very gently to suggest to Tom that he would find his work much easier if we could at least level some graves where families agreed to it. I knew he would say 'no', but hoped I'd planted a seed.

Roy let everyone know how horrified he was at the state of the churchyard. Brushing aside Tom's reaction, he wanted to see all the curbs removed and some of the awkward mounds flattened. Most people could see the sense in this and felt that, given a little more time, Tom might come round to the idea. This did not allow for a lady by the name of Miss Millicent Marchant.

Miss Marchant was a new resident. With her trim figure, long skirts and straw hats she could have stepped out of an Edwardian family photograph. She joined the church council, but sensibly decided to get herself established before saying too much. However, at this moment she could not resist venting her feelings about 'God's little acre', as she called it.

"Rector, I want you to know that at our church near Birmingham all the gravestones were taken away. Now it's a beautiful garden of rest. Think how lovely it would be here. The grass cut like a lawn, rose beds planted and seats where people could sit quietly. We could pave the path with the old gravestones and maybe hold a summer fête there, just as we did at my old church. I was talking to Mr Edwards about it only the other day and he agreed with me."

Roy sat there open mouthed. You'd have thought a thunderbolt had struck. While Tom was still struggling to find the right words to deal with such sacrilege, I jumped in and asked if her previous church was still being used for burials. She wasn't sure, so I continued.

"Thank you, Miss Marchant. Your idea is certainly interesting but perhaps a little radical for Westaleigh. We need to give your proposal a proper hearing and also consider some of the ideas Mr Edwards and others have in mind."

Still seeing danger in Miss Marchant's eyes, I added, "It would be a great pity to spoil your idea by trying to rush it through tonight."

With relief I saw Miss Marchant sit back in her chair and Roy suggested we hold a special meeting where everyone would get the chance to voice their opinions.

*   *   *

After the ordeal of the Mothers' Union this was Roy's second test. It was true Miss Marchant had said something to him about the church-yard prior to the meeting, and he had agreed that some levelling and moving of stones was needed. The rest was news to him.

For days the parish was boiling over the issue. The clergy and Miss Marchant were accused of having hatched up the whole thing. Half the members of the church council were threatening to resign. As for Miss Marchant, she was completely unaware she'd caused such a fuss. The truth came home to her when she found herself face to face with an hysterical Emily Maythorn. But eventually she did appreciate Emily's point of view that a memorial was more than just any old stone that could be taken away and incorporated into a path. Each memorial was like an open book. Each had its own story to tell.

Roy and I met early the next morning, and in our prayers we asked that something good would come out of all this trouble. We agreed that a cooling off period was needed, but in the meantime an uneasy truce hung over Westaleigh Church.

*   *   *

One hot Saturday in July Mary put a spanner in the works. At the last minute she announced she'd forgotten to tell me I was expected to spend the whole day at a Mothers' Union event at Whiteminster Cathedral. All that was required of me was simply to show my support for the work of the Mothers' Union. I reminded Mary that the Mothers' Union was also supposed to support family life, especially on Saturdays. She dismissed this and to my amazement the children agreed with her.

I was dreading it. The coach was due to leave at about nine o'clock, arriving at Whiteminster in time for a cup of coffee, after which the ladies would go off shopping, have lunch at a café, then attend a long service in the Cathedral. With a bit of luck we'd be home by eight o'clock. A whole day gone!

I was in a foul mood as I set out for the bus shelter and it was only Kitty's finger pointing at something behind me that made me turn round. Mary, picnic basket in hand, and Paul and Ann, were bent double with laughter. I'd fallen hook, line and sinker for their prank; we were going to spend the day on the beach. I would have jumped for joy there and then if Kitty hadn't been watching with such a look of astonishment on her face.

In fact it proved more than just a day of fun. At the beach I happened to meet a rather depressed looking man from Leighford, Ed Cooper, who'd just lost his job on a farm. He was looking for work to tide him over the next few months and agreed to help Tom scythe Westaleigh churchyard. All went well until Ed, standing on a grave that had been hidden for years, suddenly found himself sinking into the ground. There were adders in the hole and Ed fled from the churchyard waving his arms in terror, Tom not far behind him.

That settled it. The whole parish now agreed that drastic measures had to be taken. Late that autumn, when snakes were no longer about, a team set to work in the churchyard. They used any means they could and levelled every mound marked by a gravestone. The remaining mounds were tested for firmness and then modified in height. Where permission was given, curbs and railings were removed. Nearly everyone seemed satisfied and even Tom agreed to try 'one of they machines'.

*   *   *

Roy and I became concerned when we discovered Emily had not been seen in the churchyard. Fearing she had taken umbrage at the changes I went to see her. She told me she had been unwell and was in fact thankful for the work being done on the graves.

When we learnt that Emily was in hospital Roy and I took it in turns to visit her. She was a very sick lady with terminal cancer and had just a few weeks to live. With tears in her eyes, she asked if I would do one thing for her, bring communion to her bedside. I'll always remember the way her face lit up as I broke the bread and poured the wine.

She died not long after and was buried beside her parents. As Roy and I left the graveside I felt sad to think there was nobody left to tend the two graves.

I was wrong. I happened to go into the churchyard a few Saturdays later. To my amazement I saw a lady of about Emily's age and stature, wearing a straw hat, standing beside the grave. The figure did not move as I approached and for a moment I thought I must be seeing a ghost. Then I recognised her, it was Millicent Marchant.

Emily's grave had become Millicent's first 'open book'.

Chapter 21

Bread or Stones?

At one of our regular Monday meetings Roy was glancing through a box of old charity papers.

"Really I can't think of anything more stupid than this," Roy burst out in disgust. Picking out some of the documents from the pile he continued, "Fancy being expected to pay out an annual shilling to needy widows; to distribute red cloaks to the children of the poor; or to supply humble labourers with bread. Here's another one 'six poor families to be given threepence each at Christmas'. Hardly enough to buy a box of matches." He thrust the papers back into the box.

"I fear I may have made a terrible mistake." Roy went on, his tone becoming serious. "I think I was ordained into the wrong church. Here we are doing this sort of daft footling thing while places like Mill Chapel are packed to the rafters and brimming over with new life. I just don't think the dear old Church of England is getting anywhere."

Having started there was no stopping him.

"I admit I may have been wrong about the Mothers' Union, but what on earth did that crazy business over Westaleigh churchyard have to do with changing lives, or giving people a vision of the glory of God? All our energy seems to be spent on tiny things, things of no consequence. We find ourselves somehow locked in the past and totally ineffective in the present. I don't blame you, I just blame the system."

"Roy," I replied. "You may well think these charities are a waste of time, but remember, we have a very long history of caring for the needy. I know they may seem outdated to you, but I for one am very proud of our long history of doing just what Jesus would expect of us."

"Fine, but there are more up-to-date ways in which the church can help. Isn't that what Jesus would expect of us? We should be paying more attention to the needs of the people now, not bothering with some outdated ideas that could have come out of the Ark! It's like offering them stones instead of bread," Roy insisted.

He was right, of course. We were living in very different times. The State was playing its part in caring for people, the introduction of the National Health Service had given everyone, rich and poor alike, the chance of better health care. But there was still a generation who, rightly or wrongly, clung to the old ways.

Roy was determined to press home his point. "Only yesterday I met Bill and Mabel Waterhead. Mabel tells me she wants to get somewhere as a Christian. Ever since she made a commitment at the Jonas Young meeting she's been coming to family services at Ashenridge. She says she doesn't feel as though she really fits in though. Now she's thinking of going to the chapel. I had to stop myself saying I'm thinking of doing the same. I honestly thought I was coming to work in some lively country churches, but there's little to show for it here."

I reminded Roy of what I'd said at our very first meeting: that country churches are not as easy as people think, and if he did decide to come here he'd be facing many challenges.

"Now here you are shying at the first fence. You know as well as I do there are free churches round here which began with a flourish, like Mill Chapel, but after a while they're struggling to survive. Have you ever thought why? I was really hoping you'd bring new ideas, enthusiasm, vision and faith to our sleepy rural churches. That's why I wanted you here as my curate."

Roy failed to appreciate what was already being achieved. I described what Ashenridge and Combe Peter churches were like when I first saw them, and how one churchwarden had even wanted to turn his church into a workshop for the disabled. I spoke of the new enthusiasm in those two churches which I hoped would gradually spread to Westaleigh. Numbers were growing at Ashenridge. At Combe Peter the family services were flourishing, thanks to people like Alice Kitson. Slowly but surely the churches were coming back to life.

Furthermore, I hoped Roy was not simply judging a church by what happened on a Sunday. Each had a long and proud history of caring for the community. Unlike some churches which rise and fall under a powerful leader, our churches had continued for centuries through thick and thin.

We managed to avoid a full-scale argument and I never doubted Roy's sincerity for one moment. It was better to get things into the open rather than let them fester.

*   *   *

About a week later Roy was getting worked up again, this time about a poor old soldier he'd visited. Ernest Kiddle lived in very simple style in a rather tired looking cottage close to the Coach and Horses in Ashenridge. His cottage contained the most basic of furniture but everything in the house gleamed with polish. Impressed by what he'd seen, Roy gradually brought the conversation round to the church. The old man told him in no uncertain terms he was through with religion thanks to all the compulsory church parades he'd been obliged to attend. Indeed, nothing would get him to a service now, especially since the church didn't even bother to deliver his Maundy loaf of bread.

Seeing me smile at this, Roy became all the more earnest. It was monstrous that a Maundy bread fund existed but was not being used.

"Roy, the last time we met you were angry about the amount of time being wasted distributing charity. Now you're angry because we've failed to deliver one loaf of bread. Before you say anything else let me tell you a few home truths about Ernest Kiddle. For a start, he's well known for being mean and miserable. After serving as a RSM in the army, he ran a very successful shoe shop in Leighford. He's actually quite well off, even though his present style of living suggests otherwise."

Roy took the point, but insisted it hadn't stopped Mr Kiddle from complaining when he'd found himself 'loafless' on Maundy Thursday. To keep the peace I promised to visit him.

Anyone calling on Ernest Kiddle did so in full view of his neighbours. Going down the 'drangway', as local people called it, armed with a loaf of bread, I was aware of net curtains twitching. I knocked at the door. I knocked again. Either his hearing had worsened since my last visit or he was deliberately taking his time. My knuckles were beginning to hurt before he finally opened the door.

"What can do I for you . . . Padre?" he asked, staring at me and then at the loaf.

Ernest Kiddle was not a man for small talk, so I came straight to the point.

"I think you know why I've come. I wanted you to have this." I offered him the loaf of bread.

"I suppose you'd better come in, Padre."

The voice was polite, the eyes impenetrable. I felt like a mouse stepping into a trap. I placed the loaf on the kitchen table. Hoping to shame him I said, "I'd heard you were in need of bread, so here it is."

My explanation about rationalising the ancient charities was politely received at first, but I could see things were not really sinking in. I went on to tell him that if he was really in need, he should come and see me and we might be able to help him from our limited funds. I knew I was on safe ground here. A former RSM and retired trader would hardly come cap in hand to the rectory.

"I was expecting this Maundy bread months ago. Why's it taken you so long?" His voice was demanding.

I went over everything again, this time at full volume. I made it very clear there would no longer be an automatic distribution of bread. If he was genuinely in need he was welcome to come and ask for a loaf.

"No more loaves," he roared, his face contorted, his moustache

141

twitching. "You think you're something special, you Padres . . . but you're nothing, nothing but drunkards, the lot of you."

Drunkards? Could he be thinking of certain army Padres he'd met. I'd met them, too. Chaplains who'd come from sheltered backgrounds, who were expected to cope with the sights and sounds of war which would turn the stomachs of the toughest of men. Some of them had turned to drink, and no wonder. My thoughts were interrupted as the tirade continued.

"How dare you take away my loaf of bread. I'll turn the whole village against you. Don't you ever have the nerve to come to this house again..."

I was half expecting the loaf of bread to hit me in the back of the neck as I walked down the path. A few of his neighours, supposedly busy in their gardens, had obviously overheard the whole thing and were doubled up with laughter. One winked at me and jokingly asked if I'd left my bread van round the corner? Another one suggested a stiff drink at the Coach and Horses might do the trick!

I walked home with mixed feelings. On the one hand laughter brought great release, and I'd certainly laughed along with his neighbours. But deep down I felt ashamed of my behaviour.

*   *   *

Roy enjoyed the account of my visit to Ernest Kiddle. Futile though some aspects of Anglican life might seem, he was also realising that, thanks to the status of the Church of England, he had unquestioned access to every home in all three parishes. His Bible study circle was attracting more and more people, and Mabel Waterhead had been one of the first to join.

Roy had also established a friendship with Harold Deane, the leading light of the Mill Chapel. At one stage he was toying with the idea of the two churches pooling their resources and running a combined youth group. He then discovered Harold would only co-operate if everything happened on chapel premises. This meant the family services which were beginning to bring new faces into our churches would lose their main support. Roy also sensed that Harold did not particularly want him to be involved in any of the teaching. So the two men went their separate ways. Harold to his warm, packed chapel, Roy to his small congregations in vast chilly buildings.

*　　*　　*

A few months later Roy became concerned when Mabel stopped coming to his meetings. We then learnt that Bill was in Whiteminster Hospital with a broken leg so assumed his wife would be busy visiting. Nothing could have been further from the truth. As a self-employed man Bill had no sick pay coming in. This meant Mabel was finding it hard to make ends meet and she had to do odd jobs as and when she could. She had neither the time nor the money to make frequent visits to the hospital.

I put Mabel's case to the two churchwardens who shared my responsibility for the use of charity money and it was agreed to cover the cost of her hospital visits from the fund.

*　　*　　*

When someone told me that Ernest Kiddle was in fact Bill Waterhead's uncle I could well imagine his reaction if he'd learnt where the money for his Maundy loaf was being spent. There was no doubt in my mind that Mabel and Bill were a deserving case and that charity should begin at their home.

Chapter 22

Sweet And Sour Music

If only things had lasted! It was always a pleasure to take the odd service at the neighbouring church of Brookworthy when its rector, James Steadman, was on holiday. Each service I took there was well supported by a congregation which really entered into the spirit of things. No suggestion here that every country church was dying on its feet.

Tom Western, the organist, loved his music. He'd sat at the same organ for over thirty years. Once he'd handed over the running of the farm to his son he could be heard playing the organ on weekdays as well. If anyone happened to come into the church while he was playing, Tom would ask if they had a favourite they'd like to hear. What's more, he never minded changing a hymn for the benefit of a visiting preacher like me. He had a knack of knowing exactly what people liked and would do his best to provide it, especially for special occasions. He was the model village organist.

Tom didn't confine his activities to the church. He was often asked to play at concerts in surrounding villages where he excelled on the accordion. He had a very easy way with everyone and was well liked. For years he'd dreamed of starting a children's choir at Brookworthy, and his dream was about to come true. A group of youngsters at Sunday School were showing promise and Tom was planning a weekly choir practice. In a year or two the choir stalls would be filled just as they used to be.

Sadly, it never happened. One evening Tom was found dead on the farm. A sudden heart attack ended his life prematurely. It was a blow to people for miles around. It was only after he was gone that everyone really appreciated all he had done, and that was more than simply playing music.

*   *   *

Things could not have been more different on my next visit to Brookworthy. I found a congregation trying to keep up with taped hymns sung by a cathedral choir. Some of the hymns were difficult, some unknown, and to make matters worse the recording crackled. During the last hymn, fortunately a well-known one, the machine gave up altogether, and with relief we carried on without it.

Not long after this I received a phone call from the bishop's secretary. She told me that James Steadman was leaving, and the bishop intended adding Brookworthy to my collection of parishes. Since the bishop had recently sent me Roy Edwards, I was well staffed and in no position to refuse his request, even if I'd wanted to. I found myself looking forward to taking a relatively lively parish under my wing.

Roy was delighted to hear about Brookworthy. His face lit up as he spoke of the young people there.

"They might swell the numbers attending our Youth Club. And we might be able to make good use of the teachers who run the Sunday School. I believe they have a good Bible study group as well . . . they might want to join my weekday group."

I turned on Roy and told him we were not looking for rich pickings like some kind of trophy hunt. Brookworthy was an active parish in its own right and must be treated as such.

"If we can't become part of their community, then I fear we will achieve very little," I concluded.

Roy took the point, but one day he would make me eat my words.

On the first Sunday Brookworthy officially joined us, people from all four parishes turned up to make it a special occasion. The church was packed. Our organist from Ashenridge played a wonderful selection of hymns and everyone sang with gusto. This was, of course, a one-off. The next Sunday we were back to singing unaccompanied. This proved better than using recorded music, but it was heavy going and left most people feeling dispirited. We had to face the fact that the congregation was beginning to dwindle and the future looked bleak. Deeply concerned, I spent a long time in the church one morning praying that we resolve the problem sooner rather than later.

*   *   *

Miraculously, the problem was resolved a few Sundays later when Lilian Bright, who sometimes attended the chapel in Ashenridge, stayed behind after the service and hesitatingly offered to play the organ. She'd heard of our dilemma and hoped she could help.

"Mind you, 'tis all self-taught," she pointed out.

The first Sunday she played 'Onward Christian Soldiers, followed by 'The Lord's My Shepherd' to the very popular tune of 'Crimond'. We did not have the words for this in our books, but most people knew them off by heart. We ended at lunchtime with 'Now the day is over', which seemed a little premature, but everyone sang lustily and it was wonderful to hear the organ being played again.

Gradually she mastered quite a number of well-known hymns. She had tremendous enthusiasm, her family supported her, and you could tell she was enjoying her new role. The parish was delighted, and things began to look up again.

It was not long before Lilian progressed to playing some of the simpler chants for the shorter Psalms. Then at Christmas she got various friends to join her family to make up a choir. They were superb. Not only did they sing in church, they organised carol singing round the parish. They tried to reach every house, and this really was appreciated. They also raised a good sum of money and insisted we add it to our church repair fund. The evening ended at Lilian's home where she'd laid on a delicious supper.

*   *   *

What followed next I write about with much pain because, unwittingly, it came about through me. A week or so after Christmas a friend of Mary's rang to say she'd just got married and would love us to meet her husband. Not only did they accept our invitation to come to tea, they also wanted to be at the evening service, which on that particular Sunday happened to be at Brookworthy.

Ellen and Peter Drummond lived in a wealthy London suburb. Over tea he spoke in condescending terms about country life and what he supposed he would find in our churches. He bragged about the huge congregation at his local church. From the list he reeled off, almost every profession was represented in that congregation. He himself was a senior accountant, and when nothing much was going on at the golf club he might well be seen in church.

That evening they sat in what's fondly called the 'Rectory Pew'. I noticed his surprise when he saw the number of people coming into the church. During the last hymn he made sure people could see he was putting something substantial into the collection bag. He needn't have bothered – in those days nobody in our congregation could ever spare a £5 note!

Uninvited, Peter followed me into the vestry. He watched quietly as the collection was counted, then after the treasurer had gone turned to me and said, "You know Jack, you really are a brick." I wondered what on earth was coming next. "I mean, coping with that awful organist. I've never heard such a terrible dirge. Where on earth did you find her? If this was my church she'd have been fired long ago."

I was about to put Peter firmly in his place when, to my dismay, I noticed the treasurer had not shut the vestry door. I could see Lilian outside piling up the hymn books. Too late, the harm had been done. I'll never forget the look on her face. Before I had a chance to speak she was gone.

I turned on Peter. "You blithering idiot, you've just sacked our only organist." I was so angry I couldn't say another word. Quite frankly I was glad to see the back of him, and he and his wife left after a brief word with Mary.

147

I couldn't get Lilian's face out of my mind. Mary said she felt partly responsible for what had happened and wanted to come to Lilian's with me. Her husband answered the door and told me she felt the only thing she could do was give up now that she knew what I really felt about her playing. Mary and I returned to the rectory in silence. We couldn't let it end there.

Next morning we went round and tried to make it clear that it wasn't my opinion but a mere outsider's whom I'd only met that day. Poor Lilian was too tearful to take it in. Several members of the church council called and pleaded with her to change her mind. Each time she replied that she was not taking umbrage, she just felt that whatever anyone said, her playing could never come up to standard.

*   *   *

While Lilian had been playing, her enthusiasm had encouraged others to come to church again. Once she left, we reverted to singing unaccompanied and numbers began to dwindle. Sometimes Roy or I would bring over an organist from another church, which did help to brighten the services.

I was deep in thought preparing a sermon for the following Sunday when Mary put her head round the door and said a Miss Cooling had come to see me. A tiny woman with a crotchety face, Miss Cooling spoke as if she'd been going to church every Sunday of her life. I couldn't recall ever having seen her at any of our parish churches, but the fact was she could play the organ and had come to offer her services. I was in no position to say anything other than 'yes'.

Unlike her predecessor, Miss Cooling had very rigid ideas about the music she would use, and even stronger views about those she would not. It was such a pity that this latter category included many people's favourites. Hence we found ourselves singing 'Guide me O Thou Great Jehovah' to some obscure tune because she disliked the one everybody knew. Miss Cooling preferred to select her own hymns and, once chosen, they could not be changed. Roy discovered this for himself when she insisted that his sermon on 'The Peace that passeth all understanding' should be followed by 'Fight the good fight'. What was more, she played this to a tune neither he nor the congregation had heard before.

The crunch came when we had a funeral at which the family requested 'The Old Rugged Cross'. Miss Cooling flatly refused to play it because she regarded it as 'hackneyed'. Against her wishes I had to bring in another organist. I eagerly awaited her letter of resignation.

But Miss Cooling did not resign. She was made of tougher stuff. Instead, she decided to make it her mission in life to educate the present generation of clergy to appreciate her high taste in music. She could not stop families asking for what she considered rather vulgar music for weddings and funerals, and on these occasions she would be happy for another organist to play.

*   *   *

There was one ray of hope. Charlotte, Lilian's eldest daughter, came to see me one evening. A pretty girl, and so like her mother with her rosy cheeks and long dark hair, she and her fiancé wanted to get married at Brookworthy Church.

Charlotte explained the reason that Lilian had not been in church had nothing to do with the organ. It was because she'd been taking her ailing mother to chapel on Sundays. Now the old lady was in hospital and not likely to live much longer. That was why they wanted to have the wedding brought forward, while her grandmother was still alive.

Guessing Lilian would be in church to hear the banns being called I specifically asked for one of her favourite hymns, 'For all the Saints'. Miss Cooling agreed to play it, but as usual refused to use the music everybody knew. This was a great pity, but at least Lilian might now appreciate our problem.

*   *   *

Roy wanted to know if I was going on the Brookworthy Church outing to Badgermouth. He and Lucy were booked elsewhere that day. I knew Mary and the children were off on a long-promised visit to Whiteminster, so that just left me. I could see myself arriving on a Saturday, trying to fill in the long hours until the coach reappeared several hours later. I began to make excuses, but Roy reminded me of what I'd once said: "If we can't be a part of their community, then we will achieve very little."

On a rather dull Saturday in June I found myself joining the Brookworthy folk and their friends on the coach. There was only one vacant seat, and I found myself sitting next to a surprisingly talkative Miss Cooling. The sharpness had left her voice and she sounded excited. Like me, this was her first experience of a Brookworthy Church outing. She'd not been to Badgermouth since she was a child, well before the First World War. She spoke of a long lost golden age, of bathing machines, fairground organs, which surprisingly she did not seem to consider vulgar, brass bands, and Punch and Judy shows. She went into raptures about all the happy times she'd spent there with her parents.

Her mood changed as she talked of a stillborn sister and her mother's death. There were tears in her eyes as she told me about her father's suicide. Her happy childhood came to a sudden end.

Suddenly the sharp voice I'd come to know returned. "The aunt who came to look after me was cold and distant. She didn't want to be bothered with me and was only fulfilling a duty. She hated me, and I grew up hating her."

I was beginning to understand something of Miss Cooling's past, but before I could say anything her face brightened and, looking out of the window, she said, "Oh look, Mr Longfield, it's turning into a nice sunny day."

There was hardly a cloud in the sky as the coach pulled into Badgermouth. I was thinking of asking Miss Cooling to join me for a cream tea in the Copper Kettle, but before I had a chance we were shepherded by some of the menfolk to a pre-selected breakwater. We paid 1/- each for a deck chair and made ourselves comfortable while the children changed into their bathers. They screamed with laughter as they ran in and out of the waves, and at that moment I wished Paul and Ann were here with me.

Then six well-known church members dressed up in disguise. If the children thought they had found one, they had to ask the question: 'When did you last have a bath?' as a kind of password. One Sunday School teacher posed as an artist and soon gathered an admiring crowd round her, while another pretended to be a council worker picking up rubbish on the beach and putting it in a big bag. She was soon surrounded by people giving her all their picnic papers. One churchwarden dressed up as an old lady with her knitting and joined Miss Cooling and some other elderly women in a shelter. He told them what was going on and there were shrieks of laughter every time a child went near them.

I'd never seen such a change. Miss Cooling chatted with everyone, and after a picnic lunch helped organise a sand castle competition. She treated the children to ice creams and they persuaded her to join them for a paddle. By mid-afternoon it was so hot I needed to get in the shade, a golden opportunity to invite Miss Cooling for that cream tea. I knew that somehow she'd left the bad times behind as we chatted about all the good things in life. We laughed together and, for the first time, I felt completely at ease in Miss Cooling's company.

As we travelled home everyone agreed the outing had been a huge success, and I kept saying to myself "thank goodness I didn't miss it."

*   *   *

The day at Badgermouth transformed my relationship with Miss Cooling. Now I knew her better I was able to tease her. I never let her forget that she herself had once loved the 'vulgar' tunes from the fairground organ.

Lilian did come back to Brookworthy Church. We worked out a rota so that she and Miss Cooling could share the duties of organist. In time they became very good friends. Lilian learnt a lot from Miss

Cooling, and Miss Cooling became more flexible when it came to the choice of music.

I'd know exactly how to approach her the next time we were asked to play 'The Old Rugged Cross'.

Chapter 23

Groucher Marx

Despite the absence of a moustache, Bruce Stanning bore an uncanny resemblance to Groucho Marx. Unlike the real Groucho, Bruce lacked any sense of humour, he complained about everything and wore a permanent scowl on his face. No wonder he'd been nicknamed Groucher Marx for most of his adult life.

I was surprised to see him at the Ashenridge Church Annual Meeting. Not only did he hate the church, but most farmers would be busy lambing at this time of the year.

The secretary read last year's minutes. I thanked all those who had worked so hard for the church during the past twelve months. Then came the presentation of the previous year's accounts. The meeting was well under way, and I was asking the secretary to record a note in the minutes thanking Jack Hayman for his magnificent work on the churchyard, when I was rudely interrupted.

From the back of the hall a voice shrieked, "That's what us 'as comed 'bout, that 'Ayman, that thieving . . ." Groucher had leapt to his feet and was shaking his fist at me. "You knows what us's talking 'bout. Us wants to know why 'tis some graves get more lookin' after than t'others?"

Of all the things to complain about, Ashenridge churchyard was the least likely. Each year it looked better and better. Ever since he'd retired, Jack Hayman had spent most of his summer days there. A labour of love he called it. Unlike Tom at Westaleigh, Jack was happy to use machines for mowing, but he still had to trim round the gravestones with a sickle. Every mound was neatly cropped, he cleared weeds round the church building and frequently trimmed the hedges. It was a real joy to watch him.

Groucher's upper lip curled. "Us all knows why thikky 'Ayman makes a fortune outa they graves. 'Tis all bribery. That's what 'tis, bribery and favouritism." He pulled an oily rag from his pocket and wiped his nose. "Call thuss a well kept churchyard. I could do better m'self. Us wants to know why Jack 'Ayman's got it in for some families?"

I let him go on for a minute or two, but his outburst was becoming abusive. I rapped the table. "That's enough, Grou . . . I mean Mr Stanning. I think you've made your point."

Bruce stood there glowering. Clearly there was more to come. I asked if anyone knew of any graves getting extra attention. There was a long pause. Bruce was having difficulty containing himself and persisted in wiping his nose on the oily rag.

"Us knows what's goin' on . . . that 'Ayman spends more time on 'is own family graves than 'e should."

There was no reason why Jack should not give special attention to his family graves. After all, he was paid a very modest sum for his work. At that point Martha Holmforth raised her hand.

"I think I can explain." She sounded embarrassed. "You see certain families pay Jack a little extra so that he'll take away dead flowers, paint railings, or wash the stones clean. I must admit my family's one; my parents made provision for it in their will."

"So that's where 'tis to." Bruce's voice sounded triumphant. "They bribes the old boy. 'E keeps the rest long, so's they'll pay 'un to keep their's short. Us'd like to know 'ow much they pays 'un?" The oily rag came out again.

Before I could say this was a private matter between Jack and the families Martha pronounced, "We pay him £5 a year."

Now it all came out. At least eight families were giving him money, and I calculated Jack must be getting almost as much again as we paid him. He was probably on to a good thing, but you could hardly call him dishonest.

Chuckling could be heard throughout the hall. I promised everyone I'd have a word with Jack, and suggested we move on to the next item.

Bruce was far from satisfied. "No, us wants thuss sorted out yurr and now." His shrill voice made everyone turn around. The grease from the oily rag had done its job and the black smear above his top lip resembled a moustache.

Without thinking Mrs Batchelor cried out, "Oh look, it's Groucho Marx."

That finished it. The whole meeting fell apart, and Bruce stormed out of the hall in a rage.

*   *   *

It wasn't long before Jack Hayman heard about the meeting. "If people thinks us be making a lot of money working up there, us'll do it no more." Despite our pleading he kept to his word. Nobody could be found to take on the churchyard. Nobody wanted to suffer the same fate as poor Jack.

The grass grew higher and higher. By now it was impossible to read the word 'Stanning' on Bruce's family graves, and I was receiving bitter complaints from undertakers and the recently bereaved about the state of the churchyard. To make matters worse, Jack's own family graves continued to look neat and tidy.

*   *   *

If the rain in early June had helped the church grass to grow, it also ensured a heavy crop of hay. Later that month it turned dry and everyone was frantically busy cutting and baling a bumper crop. Having lived on a farm I enjoyed lending a hand at this time of the year.

Bruce Stanning was in trouble on his farm. His son, Rupert, had walked out after a blazing row leaving his father to cope alone. Knowing of his bad temper no one was keen to help out.

155

I rang Roy at lunchtime, and we drove over to Bruce's farm. It was a sweltering afternoon. Just inside the farm lane we could see the field where they'd been working. In the middle stood a partly filled trailer. I knew any offer of help would be refused, so we parked the car, loaded the trailer and drove it into the farmyard. Two other fields were down and ready for baling.

The sound of the tractor echoing off the buildings brought Bruce to his back door. He looked at us in disbelief, but before he had time to say anything I waded in as though it were the most natural thing in the world for him to find Roy and me working on his farm.

"Now you get the elevator. We'll soon put this lot safe."

My tactics failed. Bruce exploded. "You'm nothin' but b . . . do-gooders. Interferin' without bein' asked. Get back to yur old ladies' tea parties. That's all youm fit fur."

Having interrupted his after-lunch nap, he was now seeing us off like a couple of trespassers. "I s'pose they'm all laughin' 'bout my good-for-nothing son. He's no more than a b . . . layabout. After all us's done And 'e needn't think 'e'll get nort from us now. 'E knowed us's worked all these years to build up a family farm, and 'tis come to thuss yurr. 'E thinks us can't even throw up a bale nowadays. But us's not as old as 'e minds."

The heavy rain that had been forecast materialised and ruined Bruce's crop. This was the last straw for Mrs Stanning and she left him.

*　　*　　*

The churchyard was in a terrible state. Everyone was blaming everyone else. Jack Hayman still felt betrayed, and the Stanning family had fallen apart. All thanks to Groucher Marx.

Chapter 24

The Badger Group

That autumn the Badger News was born. Sub-titled 'For
The Parishes Of Ashenridge, Combe Peter, Westaleigh and
Brookworthy', the front cover showed a line-drawing of each of
the four parish churches, courtesy of Westaleigh's budding artist,
Wilfred Thomas. Each magazine would feature letters from the
clergy, provide the dates and times of services, contain various
news items from each parish, laughter lines for the youngsters, and
four pages of advertisements.

From the Badger News came the idea of calling our four parishes
the Badger Group. This not only gave our churches a distinct identity,
but also encouraged the different communities to arrange combined
events. In some ways the credit for this went back to the rather controversial ideas presented by Dr Parnall, but the outworking was going
to be very different.

At a meeting with the churchwardens we began to lay our
foundations. Each parish would remain quite distinct and have its own
service every Sunday, but beyond that there were all kinds of interesting things we could do together. Lucy's idea of a combined choir was
just one of them. To get things off the ground we planned a group
service for November.

We had the best part of three months to prepare for this special
event, but I had not banked on getting a letter from the bishop which
read:

'My dear Longfield, I shall be pleased to perform the dedication at your special service. There is a forthcoming vacancy at Leighford which I hope you will fill, giving your group the scope it really needs'.

I fretted and fumed all day. I'd always resisted the idea of smaller parishes being tacked on to a larger one. I was convinced that small parishes had a life and style of their own and did not need to be dominated from outside. I wanted to be given a chance to prove that several churches working together could create just as much life and activity as that of a market town. Furthermore, Mary and the family were happy here and none of us wanted to move.

Roy felt even more strongly that it would be a disaster to run the whole group from Leighford. He could see how life in our churches was gradually gathering momentum. To change all this and centre things on a market town would be a backward step. Our years of hard work would be destroyed if we were absorbed by Leighford.

We were determined to prove to the bishop what our group of country parishes was all about. We sprang into action. In addition to the first appearance of Lucy's combined choir, we asked the Mothers' Union to lay on refreshments in the parish hall after the service. Roy and Lucy between them would get the combined Sunday schools to sing; the youth group would perform a short presentation of the Feeding of the Five Thousand, and members of the bible study group would read the lessons and lead the prayers. We'd also use the occasion to revive interest in bell ringing.

*   *   *

The Group Service was just over two weeks away and everything seemed to be going to plan. That Friday evening the Youth Club rehearsed the Feeding of the Five Thousand. The rehearsal went well, but afterwards one of the youngsters asked if she could be taken home first because she had a really bad headache. This meant Roy had to reverse his route and drop Yvonne Slope off last. Ever since Yvonne had developed a crush on Roy at the Youth Club camp that summer he had taken care never to be on his own with her, but now

158

he had no choice. Having dropped off the other passengers he found himself alone with a very giggly Yvonne who insisted on sitting beside him in the front seat. Resisting any suggestions that they should stop, he got her home as quickly as possible.

When the Youth Club met again the following week, Roy was determined he would have no nonsense with his passengers. He need not have worried – hardly anyone turned up, and the rehearsal didn't take place.

A shocked Roy came to see me the following day. Evidently Yvonne Slope had been boasting at school that just before taking her home, Roy had stopped by a bridge, grabbed her and kissed her. She then claimed he only let her go after she managed to get out of his car and scream her head off.

I assured Roy that I knew Yvonne's story could only be just that, a story. I called on Mr & Mrs Slope but made little progress. They wanted to hush things up rather than create a fuss.

I realised that even if people were to give Roy the benefit of the doubt, there were always those who would say 'no smoke without fire'. If nothing was done to refute Yvonne's claims, Roy's name would be under a shadow, his excellent work ruined, and the whole future of the Badger Group would be put in jeopardy.

Help came from a completely unexpected quarter.

$$* \qquad * \qquad *$$

'Poacher Sam' was heading for the Coach and Horses when a bent figure emerged from the bus shelter and stopped him in his tracks.

"They tells me they 'ad some good salmon to the Poacher's Inn two Saturdays a-gone. Fresh 'twas and caught not far from 'ere – by the bridge where poachers go when 'tis dark. Yer knows where 'tis to. Funny thing, they says 'twas someone drivin' an old van just like yer's delivered the fish."

"Yurr, what be ye getting' at?" an angry Sam retorted. "What I does 'tis nort to do with you. Any case, you got no proof."

"Kitty knows," was all the answer he got. "There's more than that.

Yer was there when that young passon drove by, and I knows 'e never stopped there. Drove straight on and took the maid 'ome."

"So what?"

"Yer knows what they'm sayin' and tiddn' true, not a word of it. 'E never stopped there and yer've got to do somethin' 'bout it. If you don' then us'll 'ave a tale to tell. Kitty won' keep quiet unless that lyin' maid tells the truth. 'Er'll be 'ome now. Yer knows where that's to."

"You b . . . old witch. You'm nothing but an interferin' old busy-body."

"Remember what 'appens if yer don'," came the warning as Kitty hastened back to the warmth of her home.

Later that evening Yvonne found herself under heavy pressure from her parents to go round and tell the truth to all her friends. She was to make sure they all played their part at the Group Service. If she failed to do this, Sam would come out with the truth which would do irreversible harm to the good name of the Slope family.

*　　*　　*

Only three days prior to the service Mary had news of her own. Rumour had it that Mrs Batchelor was employing a professional florist to decorate the church. Furthermore, as a special 'surprise', on the Sunday evening we would find the choir stalls filled with members of Leighford Operatic Society who were going to sing selections from their latest production, The Pirates of Penzance.

Mary eased my nerves a little by saying, "Don't worry, Jack. Leave Mrs Batchelor to me."

*　　*　　*

The bishop was due to arrive at six o'clock. This would enable us to have a chat about the vacancy at Leighford, and give me a chance to reiterate my objections. Come 6.15pm he still hadn't appeared and the service was due to start at 6.30pm. With only minutes to spare, his chauffeur-driven car dropped him at the rectory and we hardly had time to exchange pleasantries before dashing across to the church.

Two beaming churchwardens greeted the rectory party as we arrived. I noticed the red-curtained Sunday School area was surrounded by a sea of flowers arranged by Mrs Batchelor's florist. As I'd hoped, the rest of the church decorations had been left to the ladies from the four churches. Lucy's combined choir was already sitting in position, and the first four pews were filled with members of Leighford Operatic Society. The bells were ringing as I'd never heard them before.

Much to my relief the Operatic Society joined with the combined choir to give an outstanding rendition of the Halleluiah Chorus. I knew Mary had done her stuff and my worries about The Pirates of Penzance disappeared. After the bishop had dedicated the Sunday School area, the children entered, each wearing a buttonhole of flowers. Finally, the Youth Group performed the Feeding of the Five Thousand. This brought a huge round of applause, and Roy's face was radiant.

In his address the bishop enthused about the Badger Group being a very promising sign for country churches of the future. I couldn't help thinking if that was the case why would he want to change things now. To Mrs Batchelor's delight he described the newly dedicated area at the back of the church as a 'splendid refectory'. From that moment on Len Cooksley insisted on calling it the 'suspended rectory'!

After the service Mary had to collect a couple of things from the house. Unobserved, she passed behind some parked cars and recognised two familiar voices. An angry Peter Eastridge was holding forth about cars blocking the village. "I knows all about it. That b . . . lazy rector's got his way with the bishop. You wait and see, it'll be just one service for all the parishes. He'll be closing the other churches."

To her delight Mary heard Jim Stillman reply, "All I can say is I've never seen so many people going to church. Whatever his faults, our rector seems to be doing a good job. For what it's worth!"

*   *   *

161

The parish hall had been beautifully decorated with flowers for the celebration, another surprise from Mrs Batchelor. Mrs Mock was in her element helping to serve a selection of sandwiches, jellies and cakes, all provided by members of the Mothers' Union.

Hearing a commotion at the back of the hall, I turned and stared in disbelief at the figure standing in the doorway. It was Uncle Tiddly, a bottle of Champagne in one hand, a glass in the other. "Congratulations, Jack. Congratulations everyone. You're doing a splendid job."

Mary's jaw dropped. I was speechless. We noticed Paul and Ann giving Uncle Tiddly a conspiratorial grin. So that was it, they'd invited him without telling us. The Operatic Society chose that moment to start singing their medley from The Pirates of Penzance. Before I could stop him Uncle Tiddly turned to the bishop, winked, and said, "I know a brilliant joke about the pirates of Penzance. Do you want to hear it?"

"Not now, dear." Mary smothered a laugh as she pulled Uncle Tiddly to the other side of the hall.

To my relief the bishop grinned. Perhaps he'd already heard it!

The whole evening was full of surprises. A young man from Brookworthy, who'd read our cry for help in the Badger News, said he'd be happy to mow Ashenridge churchyard. Kitty proudly told me she'd given up 'they ciggies'. And Desmond, who could have ended up in such trouble, was busy chatting to the bishop about Roy and his Youth Group.

I looked round the packed hall at all the familiar faces. Mabel and Bill Waterhead, Trevor and Margaret Broadford, two couples who'd certainly had their fair share of problems but had come to know the joys of marital bliss. Lovely Alice Kitson who, despite being hard of hearing, was tapping her feet to the music. And Lilian Bright and Miss Cooling chatting nineteen to the dozen over a cup of tea. There were so many of them and I was fond of them all. They were my friends. I may not see all of them in church every Sunday, or on any day for that matter, but they all played their part in the life of the parishes. Dear God, I thought, I'm not ready to leave here yet.

The celebration was a huge success. To show their appreciation a ripple of applause broke out as the bishop took his leave. Roy and I walked him to the car and as we said our goodbyes he turned and shook us firmly by the hand. "I see what you mean, Longfield. I'd like to congratulate you and Roy . . . I'd like to congratulate everyone on what's been achieved here. Forget what I said about Leighford. I don't think you could cope with Leighford as well."

Mary and I made sure everything was safe at the hall, turned off the lights and strolled back to the rectory as if walking on air. Paul and Ann were in the kitchen laughing with Uncle Tiddly, who produced yet another bottle of Champagne. Mary grabbed an assortment of glasses from the dresser and we drank a toast to the bishop, to all the parishes and last, but not least, to friendship.

*　　*　　*

I was in great spirits the following day. Colonel Waters made an unexpected visit and we laughed as he reminisced about the first time we met and how alarmed he'd been by my forthright views.

"You know, Jack, I realise now that I was trying to hang on to a church with a golden past. I've learnt through you that the church does have an exciting future." With a smile he added, "But I think you'll agree it's been tough going some of the time, rather like this hymn."

He passed me the hymn book and pointed to these words:

> 'Not for ever in green pastures
> Do we ask our way to be;
> But the steep and rugged pathway
> May we tread rejoicingly'

Chapter 25

It Really Was Christmas

The Badger Group Service may have been the climax of my first six years at Ashenridge, but the most dramatic and moving event was still to come.

In March that year a young man by the name of Dick Carter had been charged with the attempted murder of a policeman and detained in Bristol's Horfield Prison. Fearing reprisals, the authorities re-housed his wife, Sheila, and their two sons in Ashenridge, where they kept very much to themselves.

By sheer chance Roy discovered who they really were on his very first visit. Sheila had left a pile of newspaper cuttings on the kitchen table and every one of them referred to a Dick Carter.

AXE MAN
LEAVES POLICEMAN IN A COMA

A father of two who attacked a policeman as he radioed for help has been accused of attempted murder . . . Dick Carter, 34, of Bristol was found at the scene of the crime holding a blood-stained axe . . . The policeman, who had received several blows, remains in a coma. Carter has been remanded in custody at Horfield Prison.

In truth, Sheila was desperate to talk to someone she could trust and as Roy scanned the cuttings he noticed her hands shaking and she was close to tears.

Roy and I did our best to help the family and after a lot of persuasion they started to join in and Tommy and Matthew came to Sunday School. But it was inevitable word would get round in a small parish like Ashenridge and, sadly, some parents shunned the family. Sheila climbed back into her shell. That autumn Tommy had his fifth birthday, but it was Mary who took him to and from school.

Dick never ceased protesting his innocence. On that fateful day he'd decided to take a break before making his last few deliveries. It was getting dark as he drove his white transit van into the lay-by. A black van was pulling out, but he thought nothing of it until he discovered the wounded policeman slumped in his car. Of course he had blood on his hands, he'd tried to help. And yes, he was holding a blood-stained axe, but he couldn't remember why he'd picked up. When the emergency services arrived things looked bad for him.

Having met Dick and listened to his version, Roy and I knew he was no 'axe man'. Everything hinged on the colour of the transit van. Before losing consciousness the policeman had managed to radio for help and gasped the words 'transit van'. Not black, not white, just transit van. Unless he came out of his coma there was no hope of proving Dick's innocence.

Sheila had never doubted her husband for one minute knowing him to be a loving husband and wonderful father. I'd only seen her break down once. I was driving her to Bristol for a prison visit and she'd suddenly clasped her face in her hands and sobbed, "If that policeman dies, if he dies, Dick could be accused of murder, couldn't he, Mr Longfield? Dick could be hanged for that."

She confided to me that in her dreams Dick was running up the garden path, but she always woke up before he reached the house. That was why she'd taken to leaving the key in a safe place ready for his return. Only he and one other person, Will Swift, knew where it was hidden.

*   *   *

165

As the festive season approached Ashenridge became a hive of activity. For the very first time we were planning a Christingle Service on Christmas Eve and ideas were coming in thick and fast.

The season of good will could be felt everywhere and as the weeks went by some parents made a point of calling on Sheila. Life for the Carters gradually returned to some sort of normality, and it was good to see Sheila standing at the school gates again.

Mary and Lucy came up with a wonderful idea. "Christmas isn't going to be much fun for Sheila and the boys this year, so we're going to organise a collection and buy presents for them all."

People were more than generous and it was agreed our churchwarden, Will Swift, would slip away towards the end of the service and the parcels would be waiting for them when they got home.

*   *   *

Sheila could not afford the luxury of a phone and I'd been happy to act as a messenger when any calls needed to be made or came through about Dick.

Mary and I were about to have a Christmas Eve lunch with Paul and Ann when the call came through from Dick's solicitor. The policeman had come out of his coma, was making a good recovery, and although he couldn't remember every detail he recalled that on the afternoon in question he'd spotted a black van fitting the description of one used for a robbery. It was parked in a lay-by and before he had time to investigate a man leapt from it wielding an axe. He managed to radio for help, but beyond that his memory was still vague. When asked to confirm the colour of the van he had no hesitation in saying, "Black, it was definitely black."

Lunch forgotten, I now had to stop Paul and Ann rushing out to spread the good news and swore them to secrecy. Sheila must be the first to know. The solicitor rang again. There was a fifty-fifty chance Dick would be released that day.

Sheila was alone when I got to the house. At first she couldn't take it in. One moment she was dumbstruck, the next she was screaming, "I

166

told you, didn't I, I told everyone Dick was innocent." As we hugged each other I offered up a quick prayer of thanks, the quickest ever. My mind was racing. The Christingle Service began at seven. Roy was taking the Midnight Service at Westaleigh. He could get to Bristol and be back in time, couldn't he? The solicitor had said 'fifty-fifty chance'. It had to be worth a try.

"What do you think, Sheila?" It had to be her decision.

"Yes please, Mr Longfield, let's try. But don't say anything to anyone yet, especially Tommy or Matthew. If their dad doesn't get back in time for Christmas it would be cruel. They're still a bit young to understand what's going on. I'll explain it all to them after Christingle.

Roy had driven Sheila to Horfield Prison on a couple of her visits and I'd hardly had time to give him the facts when he grabbed his keys and shot off in his beloved car like a knight errant. I rang the solicitor and told him what was happening. He couldn't give any guarantees but promised to do everything in his power to get the release papers signed that afternoon.

By the time Roy reached Horfield Prison Dick's solicitor had done a good job and the release took less than an hour. He had no doubts now that he'd get Dick back to his family in time for Christmas.

*   *   *

Meanwhile, back at Ashenridge Annie Cook had just finished another cup of tea and glanced at the clock again. At last it was time to go over to the church. Annie had volunteered to prepare the candles for the Christingle Service. She'd been looking forward to it all week and made sure the trays of Christingles were in their proper place at the altar rail. It took several minutes for her to light every one of them but it was worth it because in this way they would light more quickly during the actual service.

The flickering flames cast shadows round the darkening church and Annie paused for a moment. The Christmas tree was the best she'd ever seen. There were huge sprigs of holly, masses of tinsel, and even more candles waiting to be lit that evening. And as for the flowers . . . She could not remember a time when Ashenridge Church had looked *so* magnificent. She cherished the moment before bending to blow out the candles.

*   *   *

As Roy and Dick drove along the A38 towards Bridgwater their conversation was flying in all directions. Sheila, Tommy and Matthew, Christmas, catching up on all the news . . . Dick was overjoyed when he heard about the surprise presents waiting for the family. He desperately wanted to be there to see the look on their faces. They seemed to fly along the near-deserted road. Soon they'd be approaching Taunton. What a moment! This really was Christmas and Roy was enjoying his role as Santa Claus.

One moment they were happy in conversation. Next, the steering faltered, the road became uncomfortably bumpy and the car started pulling towards the hedge. Roy managed to steer it into a gateway but that was it, a flat tyre. He had no torch, and for some stupid reason the spare wheel was in his garage at home. They were stuck on a darkened road, miles from Ashenridge and not a soul in sight. Roy and Dick stared at each other in disbelief. So near and yet so far. There was only one thing for it, they'd have to start walking and hope someone would stop and give them a lift.

They waved their arms frantically as two cars approached. Both drove past without stopping. Minutes later another car's headlights came into view and pulled up alongside them. The driver stuck his head out of the window and Roy found himself staring at a well-built man smelling strongly of alcohol. Thank God he knew where Ashenridge was.

"As a matter of fact I'm heading that way myself," he said. "Just a minute, don't I know you? Well I'll be . . . you're the young parson who works with Jack Longfield. You may not remember me, but we met at the Group Service celebration only last month. Uncle Tiddly's the name. Hop in and tell me what the devil you're doing this far from home on Christmas Eve."

168

As the story unfolded Uncle Tiddly whooped with delight.

"Time to celebrate," he cried, pulling a miniature whisky bottle out of his pocket. "Here have some of this, it'll keep out the cold. Go on fellows, have a good swig. I've plenty more. Always bring a good supply with me when I'm staying at Jack's you know."

One bottle after another came out of his pockets and Roy wondered how long it would be before he became incapable of driving.

"Here, have some more. Cheers!" Roy downed another drink but decided to make it his last. He wouldn't look good swaying before the congregation at Westaleigh's Midnight Service, reeking of alcohol and slurring his words.

Dick didn't need a drink. He was already drunk with happiness. The nightmare was over and he'd soon be reunited with his family.

"So, Dick, what do you think your family will say when they see you?"

When he heard the plan about the presents being taken to the house he whooped with delight again. "That means I'm delivering the best present of all. I'm Father Christmas! But we must do things properly, and we've just got time.

Without warning he drew up at a near-deserted garage, the very last of its Christmas trees spread out on the forecourt.

"I'll have that one, please." Uncle Tiddly pointed to an enormous tree that must have been eight feet high. He scratched his head. "Um, how the dickens are we going to get that in the Rover."

Together they managed to push and pull the tree through the two rear windows and fasten it with some cord. Roy kept glancing at his watch. They were pulling out of the forecourt when Uncle Tiddly screeched to a halt and reversed the car. "Can't have a tree without lights, can we. Better take both boxes."

*   *   *

By now the lights were on at Ashenridge. Len Cooksley was playing carols on the bell chimer in the tower, the music travelling far and wide on the frosty air acting as a rallying call to the bell ringers.

The church was packed and more chairs had to be set up in the 'suspended rectory' to accommodate everyone. Mary and Lucy sat with Sheila exchanging smiles. What a secret to be sharing on Christmas Eve.

*   *   *

As they sped along the A38, Roy kept checking the time. If they were lucky they could get to Ashenridge before the service ended. All three occupants of the car were shivering thanks to the chill breeze blowing through the open windows. Uncle Tiddly was already showing signs of the effects of 'keeping out the cold'. Even worse, when they'd stopped at the garage he'd restocked his pockets with a further supply of miniatures from the boot.

"Here's to Father Christmas," he chortled, helping himself before passing the bottle round. "Have you fellows scoffed the rest?" He'd no idea that Roy and Dick had been hiding the half-empty bottles.

"There's nothing like a drop of whisky for keeping out the cold. I was all by myself last Christmas you know when I met this sweet little thing in the pub. She liked whisky, too. It wasn't long before I had my hands all round her and . . ."

"Let's sing a carol," Roy broke in before Uncle Tiddly got too carried away. First it was Jingle Bells, then Good King Wenceslas. Roy could see the whisky taking more and more effect.

At last the car turned off the A38 and headed for Leighford. As the raucous singing continued Uncle Tiddly took his eyes off the road and in that one split second the car began to swerve dangerously from side to side and they almost landed in a ditch. Uncle Tiddly was visibly shaken and didn't touch another drop for the rest of the journey. Once they'd passed the sign for Ashenridge they knew they were home and dry and let out an almighty cheer.

*   *   *

The service in Ashenridge Church was in full swing. The Nativity Play nearly turned into a disaster when it was realised nobody had brought a doll to go in the manger. Fortunately little Emily, cast as a shepherd, had her favourite doll with her. Without the little girl noticing her mother quickly handed it over.

A group of excited children re-enacted the journey to Bethlehem, the inn and the stable scenes. Sheila glanced proudly at Tommy and Matthew as they played their part. If only Dick could have seen them. All went well until it was the turn of the shepherds to visit the stable and little Emily, seeing her doll in the manger, grabbed it and shot to the back of the church. The sight of a shepherd kidnapping baby Jesus was just too much and a ripple of laughter went round the church.

As the service reached its climax Will Swift slipped quietly from the church. I held out a Christingle to the congregation explaining that the orange represented the world, the candle Jesus as the light of the world, the prickly holly with its tear-shaped berries the sufferings of Jesus, and the dried fruits the good deeds which follow when we try to live the kind of life Jesus taught us.

The lights in the church were switched off and I read the Christmas passage from St John's Gospel by the light of a single Christingle. From my one flame all the Christingles were lit and the children came up to the altar rail to receive them. The last carol was sung by candle-light.

As the service came to an end a trail of flickering candles could be seen slowly moving out of the dimly-lit church. It wound its way through the churchyard, fading into the distance as people made their way home quietly singing 'We wish you a Merry Christmas, We wish you a Merry Christmas, We wish you a Merry Christmas and a Happy New Year'.

Sheila was waiting for me by the car. I put my arm around her shoulder and whispered, "Don't give up hope." I made sure Tommy and Matthew held on to their Christingles so they could re-light them at home.

I was pulling up at the house when a car sped past going in the opposite direction. I had to stop myself from yelling out as a beaming

Uncle Tiddly waved from the driver's seat. Was I imagining things? That was Roy sitting next to him, giving me the thumbs up sign, wasn't it?

As I re-lit the Christingles my heart was beating nineteen to the dozen. Tommy and Matthew led the way in. There were shrieks of delight as the children spotted the presents. "Oh look. Look, mum, Father Christmas has been." The light from their Christingles picked out a pile of parcels, sprigs of holly and tinsel. Sheila was in tears, trying to ask who had given all these lovely presents. The children were making too much noise to hear the sound of other vehicles parking outside.

"These presents are from the many friends who have come to know you, respect you and admire your courage. One or two may have misjudged you at first, but now the whole world knows you were right."

I turned to Tommy. "See that light switch. Could you turn it on."

Dozens of sparkling fairy lights lit up Uncle Tiddly's tree, and standing behind it was the biggest, the most precious Christmas present the Carter family could ever have prayed for.

From outside a choir began singing 'O Come All Ye Faithful', and I slipped away.